# Cathy Cassidy

# BROKEN HEART CLUB

PUFFIN

PUFFIN BOOKS

UK | USA | Canada | Ireland | Australia
India | New Zealand | South Africa

Puffin Books is part of the Penguin Random House group of companies
whose addresses can be found at global.penguinrandomhouse.com.

www.penguin.co.uk
www.puffin.co.uk
www.ladybird.co.uk

First published 2016
001

Set in Baskerville MT Std 13.25/19.25 pt
Typeset by Palimpsest Book Production Limited, Falkirk, Stirlingshire
Printed in Great Britain by Clays Ltd, St Ives plc

A CIP catalogue record for this book is available from the British Library

HARDBACK ISBN: 978-0-141-37124-5
TRADE PAPERBACK ISBN: 978-0-141-37125-2

All correspondence to:
Puffin Books
Penguin Random House Children's
80 Strand, London WC2R ORL

www.greenpenguin.co.uk

Thanks . . .

As always, thanks to Liam, Cait and Cal, and to all of my lovely family. Big hugs to Helen, Sheena, Fiona, Lal, Mel, Jessie and all of my fab friends. Hats off to Ruth, my PA, to lovely Annie who arranges my tours, and to Martyn who does the numbers stuff. Thanks to Darley and his team for being generally awesome.

Special thanks to my fab editors, Amanda and Carmen; to Erin for the stunning cover artwork; and to Puffins Sam, Mary-Jane, Tania, Julia and the wonderful Roz for all the help and support.

Thanks to the original Heart Club, wherever you may be now . . . your inspiration helped to create this story. The last and biggest thank-you is for YOU, my readers . . . when the going gets tough, you guys keep me going.

 xxx

# THEN

*Prologue*

It's a Friday afternoon in late July, the summer after Year Six, and Andie and I are scrabbling about in the drizzle, wrestling with the canvas of the big old bell tent and giggling too much to actually get anywhere. Ryan from next door comes over to put up his little pop-up one-man tent and we drag him in to help, but that makes things worse because Andie is too busy flirting to take much notice of ropes and canvas. In the end Ryan goes home and Andie's dad has to untangle the mess and help us put the tent up properly.

It's Andie's eleventh birthday, and we've planned a sleepover party, a garden camp-out for the Heart Club. It's also a bit of a farewell thing, because Tasha and her family are moving to France in ten days time and Hasmita will be going to a different secondary school after the holidays.

Tomorrow Andie and her family are going to Scotland for a week's holiday, so even if Tasha's family are still here by the time she gets back, it could be the last time we all get together properly. I get a sick feeling in the pit of my stomach at the idea of us being parted.

We all know that things are changing, and none of us like it.

'It's got to be a sleepover to remember, Eden!' Andie says, peering out at me from under her anorak hood. 'It's got to be special!'

'It will be.' I promise, because our sleepovers always are and who cares if the TV says this is the wettest summer we've had in forty years? A bit of rain can't stop the Heart Club from having fun. We spread bright rugs, pillows and blankets inside the bell tent, hang battery-powered fairy lights around the inside, make raggedy bunting to liven up the inside of the tent by tying endless strips of bright fabric scraps on to the strings of fairy light. They look beautiful, in a frayed and slightly frantic way.

'OK,' Andie declares at last. 'It's my birthday, and I reckon we've earned cake. C'mon, Eden, let's go get ready – the others will be here soon!'

We head for Andie's bedroom, a tiny boxroom painted sunshine yellow and papered with boy-band posters and bright, manga style paintings she's done herself. Andie's mum is saving the birthday cake for later when Hasmita, Tasha and Ryan arrive for the sleepover, but she's given us jam tarts and cheese on toast, and Andie ramps the music up to full volume to get us in the mood.

'I think I'm in love,' Andie says, throwing her arms wide. 'Ryan Kelly. Who knew?'

'Isn't it a bit awkward falling in love with one of your best friends?' I ask.

'It's awesome, because we've known each other forever,' she says. 'We already love each other in a friend-ish way, I just have get Ryan to see I'm not just the girl-next-door. Imagine . . . all this time and I've only just noticed how cute he is!'

I smile, but I know my ears have gone pink and I hope Andie doesn't notice.

'Tonight could be the night,' Andie sighs. 'He might say something – make a move. Or maybe I will! What d'you think?'

'Cool . . . why not?' I say, even though it's not cool and

I can think of a million reasons why not. It doesn't matter, though; I don't think Andie will do anything more than flutter her eyelashes at Ryan. She's eleven; she's not ready for romance yet – any more than I am.

For me, friendship comes first anyway; I think it always will.

I reach into my sleepover rucksack, pull out a little parcel wrapped in gold tissue paper and tied with red raffia, and hold it out to Andie.

'Just wanted to give you this before the others get here,' I say, grinning. 'Happy birthday, Andie!'

'Oooh! What is it? It's tiny . . . but heavy!'

She peels the tissue paper back and lifts out a little silver heart pendant, the kind that breaks in two so that two best friends can share. Her face lights up with glee, and she holds one half of the heart pendant out to me.

'Wow! I've always wanted one of these!' she exclaims. 'Thank you. A friendship locket, right? One half for me and one for you, because you are the best, best friend ever, Eden Banks. I love you loads, and I'll always be there for you, promise!'

I believe her. Andie has always been there for me, even

through this past year. My parents split up, and I don't think I could have got through it without Andie's support.

'Any word from your dad?' she asks, as if reading my mind.

'Nothing,' I tell her. 'I think he's forgotten me.'

'Oh, Eden,' Andie says. 'As if anyone could ever do that!'

She puts on her half of the heart pendant while I put on mine, and then she flings her arms around me and hugs me tight, laughing, and I can smell the vanilla scent of her shower gel all mixed up with the aroma of strawberry jam and cheese on toast.

'I love my pressie,' she tells me. 'I'm going to wear it always. Awww . . . tonight is going to be epic!'

Epic is one word for the camp-out, I guess. By midnight, the rain is sheeting down and the bell tent is full of puddles; Ryan's little one-man tent has already collapsed in a soggy heap.

It's like the end of the world, but Andie doesn't do failed sleepovers and somehow she makes it all seem cool, an adventure. We eat hot pizza with pineapple chunks and chocolate birthday cake with ice cream. Ryan has brought over his copy of *Harry Potter and the Philosopher's Stone*, which he wants to lend to Andie, but she's not in the mood to listen to chunks of story right now. She has swiped her mum's iPod and makes us all sing karaoke to dodgy, ancient cheese-pop. By the time Ryan launches into his rendition of 'It's Raining Men', we're laughing so much the tears run down our cheeks, and it doesn't matter any more about the leaky tent or the fact that fate is pulling us apart.

Andie ramps up the volume to max, opens the tent flaps and drags us out into the downpour.

'Noooooo!' Tasha is screeching. 'I'm soaked already! Are you crazy, Andie Carson?'

'I'd rather be crazy than boring,' Andie declares, pulling me and Tash out into the deluge. 'C'mon, guys, think of it as a rain dance in reverse! Who cares about a little bit of rain? Once you're wet, you're wet, right?'

'A little bit of rain?' Hasmita argues, pushing her black plaits up into a woolly hat with a grin. 'Trust you to look on the bright side, Andie! This is a monsoon, a tsunami, a hurricane . . . plus it's pitch black! Are you serious?'

'Andie's never serious,' Ryan says. 'But I am – get dancing!'

He flings himself into a full-on disco routine, playing it for laughs, and the rest of us join in, half-hearted at first and then with energy. I'm drenched, but it feels awesome, like I am truly alive for the first time in forever. I'm wearing pyjamas and a rain jacket, my feet soaked and squelching in thick socks that are already slick with mud. Trickles of cold rain slither down my upstretched arms, but I'm laughing, singing, loving every moment. I'm with my best friends. So what if it's chucking it down? We are the Heart Club, and not even the wettest summer in forty years can stop us having fun.

I'm dancing around, my arms wide like wings, doing some kind of shimmy with Andie when I slip on a patch of mud, twisting my right ankle. I gasp with pain. Andie whirls away from me in the dark, oblivious, her bare feet sliding in the wet grass, long fair hair transformed into rat's-tail ringlets flying out around her face. Tasha and Hasmita dance on too, faces turned up to the starless sky . . . they have no idea I've hurt myself. Only Ryan sees me stumble, and drops his comedy routine to come over and help.

'You OK, Eden?' he asks, and like an idiot I am blushing because he's noticed and cares.

I try shifting my weight on to the damaged foot, and red-hot pain sears through me instantly. 'Ouch,' I say. 'I can't stand on it . . .'

Ryan takes my elbow and steers me back to the tent, and I crawl inside, peeling down one squelching sock. He flicks a torch on, and in the little pool of yellow light I can see my ankle is already swelling, looking disturbingly spongy and Swiss roll-like.

A surge of self-pity rolls over me. My ankle is throbbing and sharp, shooting pains make my eyes brim with tears. The party vibe has ebbed away; I am soaked to the skin, cold to the bone.

'I've spoiled everything,' I say. 'Our last proper get together ever, and now it's ruined . . .'

'Hey,' Ryan argues. 'Nothing's ruined – this was just an accident, OK? Dancing on wet grass in torrential rain probably isn't the greatest idea ever!'

'But . . . things are changing,' I protest. 'Everything's being shaken up. What if we break up, drift apart?'

'Shhh,' he says, softly. 'Change isn't always a bad thing. And nothing is going to come between us, Eden, OK? I promise.'

The words seem laden with meaning. I feel my cheeks flame and there is a fluttering in my chest that's halfway between terror and joy. It's all in my imagination, of course . . . Ryan is talking about all of us, not just me and him.

But then his fingers curl around mine, and I don't pull away. I have never held hands with a boy before. I have never felt so happy, or so scared.

'You're shivering,' he says, grabbing a blanket to drape around my shoulders. The tip of one finger wipes the tears from my eyes, and then he leans over as if he might kiss me and I panic and turn my face away, and he kisses my ear. I think I might die of happiness.

The music ends, and there is a sudden shift in the air around me. I open my eyes to see Andie kneeling in the doorway of the tent, her face frozen, eyes like ice. An Arctic chill falls over me.

'She slipped,' Ryan is saying. 'A twisted ankle, pretty bad. I was just . . .'

He trails away into silence.

'You were just what, Ryan?' Andie asks, her voice clipped and cool. 'Getting in the way, most likely. I'll sort this. You'd better ring home, Eden, get them to fetch you. You might need an X-ray or something. Too bad.'

A new track begins to blare out of the iPod speakers, an upbeat number about it being the end of the world as we know it.

I think maybe it really is.

# NOW

## 1

## Ryan

Andie was the first proper friend I ever had. We met when we were toddlers, and the proof is there for all to see, a series of shaky smartphone videos of us crawling around in the park or sharing fruit and biscuits as we played.

We lived next door to each other, and there were just a few months between us in age, so it was inevitable we'd be thrown together. Our mums were friends, too, and we spent so much time in each other's houses that both places felt like home.

Once my mum went back to work, I spent most of the week at my gran and grandad's, where everything was neat and tidy and quiet. We took long walks in the countryside, collecting acorns and fallen leaves. Gran taught me to bake bread and Grandad gave me a little patch of his garden to grow carrots and sunflowers, and sometimes we did puzzle games together or kicked a ball around in the garden.

At the end of the day one of them would often drop me off at Andie's while I waited for Mum and Dad to get home. If my grandparents' house was quiet and orderly, Andie's was the opposite . . . noisy and hectic and warm and fun, especially after Andie's two little brothers came along.

Andie always said I was lucky, back then, getting to go to Gran's. She thought she was missing out. Then, when we were four, Andie started at nursery school, and I was the one who felt left out. I didn't go, because Gran and Grandad lived on the other side of town, and because Mum said spending lots of time with them was an education in itself.

It wasn't the same, though. I wanted to know everything about nursery school. Andie said there was a sandpit and a water table and computers, books and building blocks. There was a dressing-up box and a playhouse and an indoor slide, and every other day it seemed she came home with paintings and egg-box dinosaurs and once a frog puppet made from a Dairylea cheese triangle box, some buttons and a sock.

I won't lie; I was kind of jealous.

And then Andie brought something even more astonishing home . . . a girl called Eden Banks.

'She's my new best friend,' Andie explained. 'She can be your new best friend, too!'

The two girls looked at me, Andie with her blonde pigtails and Eden with her wonky, golden-brown fringe, her upturned nose dusted with freckles. Andie was like a sister to me . . . I knew her almost as well as I knew myself. Eden was different. Her face was solemn and serious but her mouth was already twitching into a smile. She was wearing a blue cotton dress embroidered with bright flowers all around the hem, and stripy tights in shades of pink and orange and red.

I shrugged and broke a Jammie Dodger biscuit in half and offered half to Andie and half to Eden, and that was it, the friendship was sealed.

I was four years old, and already a little bit in love.

## 2

## Eden

Best friends forever? Yeah, right.

I don't believe in that stuff any more; it's for the kind of kids who still believe in the tooth fairy and pots of gold at the end of the rainbow. They are nice ideas, but they're just not true.

I mean, look around you. You see it every day . . . sadness, loneliness, bullying, boredom. Friendships built on convenience, on fear. Kids bonded together by a shared interest in maths, or cheese and onion crisps, or desperation. It's so random.

And it doesn't last.

Yesterday you had a friend for life, but today you're

alone, on the outside looking in, wondering where you went wrong.

I sound bitter, I know, but hey.

You would be too.

Losing one best friend, that's unlucky. Losing four? Well, that's just careless.

It started with Andie, that whole best-friends-forever thing.

I was four years old. It was my first day at nursery and Andie Carson (Andrea really, but nobody ever called her that) was just about the first person I saw. She was standing at an easel, all blonde spindly plaits and blue eyes, and wearing a shiny red apron. She was painting a big sunshiny picture with swirls of yellow, gold and orange, and as I watched, she leaned over with her brush and daubed a splodge of yellow paint right on my cheek.

The paint was thick and cold and slightly gritty. I blinked and my lower lip quivered, but Andie just laughed and reached out with her brush to paint my other cheek.

'You look like sunshine,' she told me, and I started to laugh, too.

By the time Miss Miller noticed, Andie had painted my cheeks yellow and my lips red and my palms white with blue spots, and I had streaked her blonde plaits with purple, pink and green. Miss Miller hauled us off to the bathroom to scrub us clean, the two of us holding hands tightly as if we would never let go.

That was the start.

We were best friends, even then, but the first time I went over to play at Andie's house things got complicated. I thought it would just be the two of us, but when I walked into the living room there was a boy in jeans and a red T-shirt, sprawled on the carpet making a Lego tower and eating Jammie Dodgers.

'Eden,' Andie said. 'This is Ryan. He lives next door . . . he's my best friend. Ryan, this is Eden . . . she's my best friend, too.'

Ryan looked up at me, curious. I watched as he snapped a biscuit in half and offered us both a piece, and I took my half politely even though it was sticky with jam and a bit smashed up around the edges.

'Hello, Eden,' he said.

'Hello.'

I wasn't crazy about the fact that Andie had another best friend, especially a scruffy, smiley boy, but there wasn't much I could do about it. Ryan lived next door to Andie and was often at her house, so in the end I got used to him. We built a den together that summer, at the end of Ryan's garden . . . a wobbly tepee made of garden sticks and covered with climbing beans that burst into bright orange-red flowers. In the winter, when the beans died, we draped the garden sticks with polythene to keep the rain out. When it got really cold, we retreated to the garden shed and turned that into a den instead.

Ryan was OK, really.

By the time the three of us started in Reception Class, I liked Ryan almost as much as I liked Andie.

The teacher sat Andie and me at a table with two other girls. Hasmita was shy, with flashing brown eyes and an armful of silvery bangles. Tasha was kind and funny, with tumbling braided hair and an infectious giggle.

Before long, the four of us were a team. At playtimes, Ryan would hang out with us, thinking up crazy games and teasing us whenever we got too girly.

We were together as much as we could be, but Andie was

always in the middle of the group, at the centre of whatever was going on. She was like the sun, and we were like the planets, moving around her, staying close to the warmth and light.

It was Andie who worked out the name thing, too.

It was just before Christmas, the year we all turned nine, and Andie was writing our names out on scraps of paper to pull out of a hat because she had decided we should do a Secret Santa.

'We all close our eyes and pull out a name,' she explained. 'Whichever name you get, you have to buy them a Christmas prezzie. You're not allowed to spend more than a fiver . . . so everyone gets something good, but each of us only has to buy one present. Cool, right?'

'Cool,' I agreed.

Then Andie's eyes widened, and she rearranged the little scraps of paper so that Hasmita's name was at the top, mine was under it, then her own, then Ryan's and finally Tasha's.

'Look!' she exclaimed. 'I never noticed before! The first letters of our names . . . see what they spell? Look!'

We looked.

Hasmita.

Eden.

Andie.

Ryan.

Tasha.

'It spells *HEART*!' Tasha squealed.

'Exactly!' Andie said. 'How did we never notice that before? We can be the Heart Club!'

The Heart Club . . . that sounded awesome.

Ryan pulled a face, but he was a boy; what did he know? He had typical boyish tendencies; weird obsessions with football and spiders and skateboards.

'Best friends forever, right?' Andie grinned.

'Right!' we agreed. 'Forever!'

Forever sounds like a long time when you are nine years old, but trust me, it can be a whole lot shorter than you know.

3

# Ryan

We said that nothing would ever change, that nothing would ever come between us. We said we'd stick together forever, but still we fell apart.

We'd never really argued before, or not for long. Someone – Andie usually – would wade in and shake things up and pull us all together again. This time, that didn't happen. After the sleepover, we shattered into about a million pieces, and there was no way of even starting to put the pieces together again.

Andie's family moved away and new people moved in. We didn't see much of them, but they had two little girls, and sometimes I would hear them playing in the garden and be reminded of Andie.

I don't see any of the Heart Club now – not even Eden, who goes to the same secondary school as me. She's a loner, these days. I see her skulking along the corridors with her head down, shoulders slumped. She might as well have her own personal rain cloud following her about; her body language says 'keep away' as clearly as if she'd scrawled it across her forehead in black marker pen. Most people get the message and leave her be, me included.

She's a different person from the girl I knew, but then I'm a different person, too, so I have no right to judge.

What happened that summer was just too big, too awful; it turned everything upside down, left its mark on us all. My way of coping was to pretend the past had never happened. I reinvented myself as someone tougher, stronger, braver. I guess Eden reinvented herself, too, but in a slightly different way.

She turned from a girl full of spark and fun into a sad-eyed kid practically drowning in ugly, baggy uniform, and I turned from class clown into school troublemaker. I'm on report pretty much all the time and I spend more time outside the head teacher's office than in class.

I have a short temper, lately. In the past, I always had

a way of turning something bad into something funny, but after that summer my knack for finding the humour in stuff deserted me. These days, I react with anger and I don't think too much about the trouble it might get me into.

None of that seems to matter any more.

I'll never forget my first day at Moreton Park Academy. It felt like someone had torn the rug out from under my feet; turned everything upside down. I'd had the worst summer ever, and now I was trussed up like an idiot in an enormous black blazer, a starched white shirt and a stripy tie that felt like it was choking me. Mum had taken me to the barbers the week before and they'd practically scalped me; when I looked in the mirror, I looked like one of those photofit pictures of dangerous criminals they show on Crimewatch.

'Give it a chance,' Mum had said. 'It'll be a fresh start!'

There was not a single person from primary school in my form group – not one friendly face. A wave of nausea rose up inside me, and I loosened the stripy tie.

'Sort that tie out,' the teacher barked. Mr Benedict was

a PE teacher, a big, beefy bloke in a tracksuit, and he was glaring at me. 'You look like a scruff!'

'Don't feel well, sir,' I said, and loosened the tie some more. 'Can I go to the loo, please?'

'Not a chance,' the teacher said. 'You've only just got here!'

The class were watching now, wide-eyed. I stood up, a little shaky, and moved towards the door. Mr Benedict stepped in front of me, arms folded, face like thunder.

'What's your name, boy?' he asked.

'Ryan Kelly,' I said, and puked up all over his shiny new Adidas trainers. Two lairy kids on the back row began to cheer at my accidental revolt, and within seconds the whole classroom was roaring with laughter. Mr Benedict looked as if he'd like to strangle me.

Fresh start? I pretty much aced it, right?

I slammed out into the corridor, looking for an escape, and walked straight into a pale, sad-eyed girl with black hair and an armful of books. She did a double take, looking up at me through a dipping fringe, her blue eyes faintly accusing.

I glared at the weird girl and broke into a run. I didn't

stop running until I was outside the school – two blocks
away in fact. Then I slowed up, sank down on a garden
wall and put my head in my hands.

I'd worked it out by then.

The weird girl was Eden Banks.

4

# Eden

I don't need a best friend.

That sounds harsh, but so what? It's true. I am used to being alone. I mean, I get on OK with my classmates . . . there are kids I chat to, hang out with at break sometimes, text when I need to check which pages we have to answer for history homework. I don't have to sit on my own in lessons, or not much, anyhow. I can sit with a whole bunch of people at lunchtime in the school canteen, if I want to.

Usually, I don't want to.

The thing is, when you let people get too close, you end up getting hurt.

You might not even see it coming.

I didn't know that when I was eight or nine, of course. I thought I was the luckiest girl alive . . . I had the four best friends in the whole known universe. We had so much fun. I try not to look back at all that, not now, but it's true. We did.

The Heart Club had the best sleepovers in the world, always. When we were at Ryan's house there would be takeaway pizza and skateboard competitions in the garden, and cheesy Disney films with talking dinosaurs and woolly mammoths and mermaids and girls who turned out to be secret princesses or warriors or heroes.

Ryan always ordered cheese and pineapple pizza, extra-giant size. That was good because Hasmita and Tasha were veggie, and I liked any kind of pizza at all – but the reason Ryan chose cheese and pineapple was because it was Andie's favourite food ever.

I noticed early on that he picked the chunks of pineapple off his own slices. 'What are you doing?' I asked.

'Pineapple – yuk!' He grinned. 'I hate it!'

'So why not order a different kind of pizza?'

Ryan's eyes slid to Andie, who was hoovering up a second slice. 'Isn't this the best thing you ever ate?' she sighed. 'Cheese and pineapple pizza. What an invention!'

That was why Ryan ordered the same pizza every time; he wanted Andie to be happy. Well, we all did.

Anyway . . . sleepovers. At Hasmita's house, we'd do makeovers, with Hasmita's big sisters painting our eyes with kohl, decorating our hands with henna, draping us in silk saris shot with silver and gold. Ryan would yawn and roll his eyes and play computer games with Hasmita's brother, Sandhu. We ate the coolest food at Hasmita's house – soft, sweet naan bread, spicy dhal and curry that made your taste buds explode.

We'd whisper our dreams and secrets long past midnight, giggling in our sleeping bags and watching the dawn light creep through the curtains.

At Tasha's, the food was wholemeal and slightly scary, but Tasha's mum would make us apricot flapjacks and veggie kebabs and burgers made of strange things like tofu and Quorn. There was no TV at Tasha's house, but her mum was a drama teacher at a college in town, and she let us loose on her boxes of props and costumes. We'd dress up as royalty or pirates or gypsies, and put on wild plays that went on for hours while Tasha's parents and their friends sat round the kitchen table, sipping herb tea and laughing, asking for an encore.

My place was a first-floor flat in an old Victorian semi, and the sleepovers there always involved baking – jam tarts and muffins and huge, towering cakes layered with fruit and cream and icing. We had a big kitchen with a huge pine table in the centre.

'We could make chocolate cake,' Andie said, the first time she saw it, and my mum laughed and helped us to make a soft, dark sponge that tasted awesome.

Later on, Mum trusted us to bake by ourselves, and never seemed to mind if we left the kitchen littered with mixing bowls, the counter dusted with flour and spattered with jam.

'Delicious,' she'd tell us, even at the start, when all we could manage was burnt biscuits and sponge cakes that sagged in the middle.

Sleepovers at my flat meant stuffing ourselves with cake and then working off the sugar high by playing on the trampoline in the shared back garden till it got dark. Later, we'd curl up in my room and watch DVDs – teen movies and chick flicks that made Ryan groan, even though he liked them secretly.

'Watch and learn,' Andie used to say. 'You'll learn loads about girls and how they tick, and that will come in very handy later in life.'

Ryan snorted. 'Huh,' he said. 'I'm not interested in girls, just football and Harry Potter. Don't know why I hang around with you lot, really. The Heart Club! You girls and your mushy films and your Indian feasts and chocolate cake and plays and make-up . . .'

He never got to say any more than that, because Andie walloped him over the head with her pillow, and the rest of us joined in until we'd battered him into submission.

'OK, OK,' he admitted, laughing. 'I like the films. A little bit. And I like the cake and the plays. But definitely not the make-up, right? And just for the record, I am really *not* interested in girls. Not yet. Yuk!'

Ryan pulled a silly face and everyone laughed, and the pillow fight was over.

The best sleepovers of all were the ones we had at Andie's house, of course. They were chaotic and crazy, and there were no food feasts or extra-giant pizzas or cool iced cakes – it was more likely to be jam sandwiches on sliced white bread, but jam butties had never tasted so good.

At Andie's, we didn't even get to sleep in the house, because she had two younger brothers and Andie's mum said we stayed up too long and made too much noise, and kept the little ones awake. So Andie's dad dragged an old bell tent down from the attic, and pitched it at the end of the back garden, and from then on, whenever we went for a sleepover at Andie's we camped out.

We loved it.

We'd tell ghost stories in the dark; spooky, scary, blood-thirsty stories of headless horsemen and zombie teachers who might lose the plot and strangle you right in the middle of a spelling test. We'd shriek with laughter and squeal with horror and make daisy-chain bracelets with quivering fingers. I always had to make Andie's, because she could never get it right.

'I don't believe in ghosts,' I remember saying, bravely, one night. Ryan had just finished telling an especially chilling tale about a boy who'd drowned in the local river and had been taking his revenge ever since by luring local children into the water so he could pull them under to their doom. It was a river we all liked to swim in on hot summer days, so Ryan's story really spooked us.

'It's all rubbish,' I went on. 'We just like scaring ourselves. There's no such thing as ghosts!'

'There might be,' Andie's voice came out of the darkness. 'We just don't know. He could be among us right now, the boy from the river, looking for his next victim, ready to lure them to a watery grave . . .'

There was the sound of a gate clanking somewhere in the distance, and we just about jumped out of our skins, screaming so loudly that Andie's dad opened the window and yelled at us to be quiet.

'How will he lure us?' Hasmita asked in a whisper.

'Jam butties, most likely,' Andie said, and Ryan laughed and threw a few jammy crusts at her and the whole thing ended up in a midnight jam fight.

We had good times; we really did.

I wish they could have lasted forever.

5

# Ryan

I have an appointment with the school counsellor. Clearly, this is the highlight of my week, the thing I look forward to more than anything. I slump on the soft chairs outside Mr Khan's office and fold my report sheet into an origami paper crane.

Andie had a craze for making them, back in Year Six. She made the rest of us learn. It took forever to master the technique, but once we'd got it, it was there to stay, like learning to ride a bike. It's a skill that comes in handy sometimes, for disposing of homework, tidying up report sheets, turning school letters into objects of beauty. I tweak the paper crane's wings and lean over to perch it in the foliage of the Swiss cheese plant next to the chairs.

Teachers keep asking to see my report sheet and I keep saying I've lost it, but if they just opened their eyes and looked around them they would see those report sheet paper cranes all over the school. No big mystery.

The office door opens and Mr Khan appears; young, nervous, adjusting his hipster glasses to see me more clearly.

'Ryan!' he says, as if greeting a long lost friend. 'Come in! Take a seat.'

I flop down on an office chair, scuff the toe of my trainer against the scratchy nylon carpet tiles.

'Good week?' he asks.

It's a trick question, of course, so I don't bother with an answer. He knows exactly what kind of a week I've had; my teachers keep him informed of my every move, and let's face it, this week has been an especially eventful one.

On his desk is a fat file with my name on the cover, and sure enough, he opens it and frowns.

'So . . . some problems, it would seem, Mr Kelly,' he says. 'A catalogue of disaster, in fact. Sent out of Miss Robson's French class for failing to hand in yet another

37

homework – that's four in a row, Ryan. It's the same story with English, maths and science. You're a bright boy, but your grades have been awful this year. Your teachers think you've given up.'

'My dog Rocket eats homework,' I shrug. 'Shreds it and chews it to a pulp. Sometimes he actually swallows it whole, especially if it's maths, but that gives him indigestion. Understandable, I suppose. It's a problem . . .'

'Ryan, this is no joke,' Mr Khan says. 'I've been speaking to your parents, and they are very concerned!'

That's a low blow. My parents are worried sick about me, I know, but they don't understand. They want to help, but how can they? Nobody can. I don't want to talk about stuff; I don't want to be counselled. I just want to find a way to forget it all, and in the process I've acquired a bad boy reputation and a bunch of thuggish mates.

I ended up being friends with Buzz and Chris, the two kids from the back of the class who'd cheered when I chucked up on my form teacher's trainers on the very first day of term. Buzz and Chris are borderline delinquents, but they make me laugh, provide me with endless distraction and a free pass to hang out with the school lowlifes. If

I'm playing footy with Buzz and Chris, I forget about my anger for a while, forget about the past. I switch off my mind and pour my energy into the game, or allow myself to get roped into their dodgy pranks and schemes. That often lands me in trouble, but so what? It's not like we're doing anything really bad. Not most of the time.

My parents, however, are not impressed.

School work dropped off my radar two years ago. I couldn't care less what marks I get because none of it matters at all. You can work your socks off at school and it still doesn't stop bad things from happening. I know that for a fact. So why bother?

Eden is just about the opposite of me; she haunts the library these days, gets top marks in every test, but I think she knows as well as I do that she'll never find the answers she needs in the pages of a text book.

'Then there was that incident in PE on Tuesday,' Mr Khan is saying. 'Although why Mr Benedict thought it was wise to give you a javelin I will never know . . .'

'Mr Benedict is an idiot,' I say.

'This is serious,' Mr Khan growls. 'You threw a school javelin over the hedge and into the garden of an old age pensioner. It landed right in the middle of her fish pond, I've been told. We're lucky Miss Smith isn't suing the school!'

'It was a windy day.' I shrug. 'I wasn't even aiming for her garden. I've got nothing against goldfish!'

'How about old ladies?' Mr Khan challenges. 'Do you have anything against them? You could have given her a seizure!'

'I didn't, though,' I say. 'C'mon, she was safely inside the house . . . I don't think she even noticed. It was an honest mistake – Mr Benedict didn't have to make such a big deal of it!'

'Can you blame him?'

I maintain a stony silence, because I do blame Mr Benedict, actually. He has never forgiven me for chucking up on his trainers back in Year Seven. He gets a kick from seeing me land in trouble.

The truth is, Mr Benedict had been winding me up for throwing like a wuss and Buzz and Chris were watching and goading me on. I'd wanted to show I could do it. I was angry and trying to prove a point, and I sort of overshot the mark. By quite a lot. But it had been an accident, obviously – I hadn't meant to freak out an old lady by hurling a giant spear past her living-room window. Truly.

I'd offered to go round and apologize, but the head told me he'd expel me if I set foot anywhere near Miss Smith's place. Maybe they really do think I'm a teenage psychopath; who knows?

'It was a great throw,' I reflect. 'I think I might have a talent for the javelin. Mr Benedict really should have put me in the school athletics team, but funnily enough he hasn't. I don't think he likes me much.'

Mr Khan closes his folder and leans back, exasperated. We both know that the javelin incident has caused a tidal wave of trouble for the school. Javelins have now been banned, and the head teacher has dipped into school funds to pay for the building of a six-foot fence between Miss Smith's garden and the school playing fields. As for me, I've somehow acquired lunchtime detentions every day until the start of the summer holidays.

I don't even care.

'Is there anything else you'd like to talk about?' Mr Khan asks, making one last attempt at sympathy. 'You know you can tell me anything. What's going on in that mind of yours, Ryan?'

'Wouldn't you like to know,' I mutter, but actually, I'm pretty sure he wouldn't. Nobody would.

'The summer holidays will be here soon,' the counsellor says with a sigh. 'Your parents are not happy. Your teachers are not happy. We need to turn things round, get you back on track. The head has suggested we might bring in an anger management therapist next term . . .'

I get up so abruptly that my chair skids across the carpet tiles and crashes into the desk, which just about gives Mr Khan a heart attack.

'No anger management,' I say, briskly. 'No therapist. No thank you. No, no, *no*!'

Mr Khan frowns. 'I don't think things are getting any better, Ryan,' he says. 'If you're not able to work on this, I think we'll need to call in some more support. OK. So do you have your report card? I have to sign it.'

'It's in the Swiss cheese plant,' I snap, slamming the door behind me.

6

## Eden

The bad stuff began in Year Six. My dad left; he said that things just weren't working out with Mum, that he loved us both, but he didn't want to live with us. I couldn't fathom it – does it really take eleven years to work out that you don't want your family any more? I cried myself to sleep every night for a month. It would have been longer, but it was like all the tears were used up after that, leaving me empty, hollow, numb.

Dad moved to London and my world crumbled, but at least I had the Heart Club. They understood. They knew not to ask too many questions, not to push me too hard. They just accepted that things were tough, and they loved me just the same as always. When I was with them, the sad stuff peeled away and I could be myself again; the real me.

And when I was alone with Andie, I could open up, talk about it and know she wasn't judging me. I told her when the divorce came through, about how Mum cried when she showed me the piece of paper that said 'decree absolute', about how she drank a whole bottle of wine and then threw the half-empty glass at the wall, where it shattered into pieces and left a dark stain on the wallpaper. Andie just hugged me, held me close and let me cry, and then she wiped my tears and held my hand for the longest time, the two of us lost in our own worlds, silent but connected.

Dad got a new girlfriend, Mum got a new job and life went on.

I learnt to square my shoulders and hide the hurt inside. I didn't know that that was just the start of it.

I am sitting on the squashy chair outside Mr Khan's office when Ryan Kelly comes thundering out, almost taking the door off its hinges. Ryan is not my friend these days; he made that pretty clear on our first ever day at Moreton

Park, cutting me dead in the school corridor as if he'd never even seen me before. That hurt, but I am used to his indifference now.

He looks at me, lip curling with faint disgust, then legs it off along the corridor, brushing against the Swiss cheese plant as he goes.

A perfectly folded origami paper crane, made from slightly grubby yellow paper, falls to the floor at my feet. I pick it up and look at it, remembering Andie's origami craze and how she taught us all to make the little paper birds. There's a heavy ache in my chest, as if I've swallowed a stone. I balance the paper crane on a branch and fix my face to neutral.

At Moreton Park Academy, everyone sees Mr Khan for a well-being check-up once a year. It is part of the school's ethos to support students both academically and emotionally, and I suppose it keeps Mr Khan in a job. Some of us have more frequent appointments, of course. I get to see the counsellor once a term; as far as I can tell, Ryan Kelly, the angriest boy in the school, sees him every week.

I wouldn't say it's helping, but hey, what do I know?

'Eden?' Mr Khan says, peering round the door. 'You can come in now!'

I slouch inside and sit down, studying my shoes. They're black Converse, scuffed, with fraying laces. Small spatters of mud fleck the canvas, making them look slightly sad and down at heel.

'So,' Mr Khan says brightly. 'No problems from a behaviour point of view and your grades are good. Your teachers say you are still very withdrawn, however. How are you feeling?'

'Fabulous,' I quip. Mr Khan scribbles the word in his file, failing to spot the sarcasm.

'No feelings of depression? Lethargy? Lack of enthusiasm for life?' he checks.

'No, I'm literally fizzing with enthusiasm,' I mutter. 'On top of the world.'

'How's the social life?'

'A non-stop whirl of all-night parties,' I say, and the penny finally drops; Mr Khan frowns and shakes his head.

'Eden, come on,' he says. 'You're a clever girl. You work very hard in lessons, but there is more to life than work. I wonder if you understand how important it is to have fun with friends, let loose a little?'

I raise an eyebrow, chew my fingernails.

'How have you been?' Mr Khan asks. 'How are you feeling? Is there anything you'd like to talk to me about?'

Mr Khan is a kind man, I know that. He still has the fluffy pink enthusiasm of whatever training course he did wrapped round him like an invisible superhero's cloak. He is on a mission to transform the students of Moreton Park Academy into happy, well-balanced, peace-loving teen-agers. Somebody really should tell him that it will never happen, but I am not planning to be that person.

'Eden?' he prompts. 'Is there anything you want to say?'

'Not really, no.'

Mr Khan's shoulder's slump, as if I have failed to deliver an especially important piece of homework. Too bad. Mr Khan has no idea at all. I can't open up to him, not ever. There is a wound inside me that will never properly heal, and if I pick the scab away just for him, the poison inside might come flooding out. It might never stop.

Keeping my mouth shut is the only way I know of keeping myself strong. It's self-defence.

'I'm fine,' I say into the silence. 'Really.'

Mr Khan sighs and scribbles a few notes in his folder.

'School closes for the summer next week,' he tells me, as if I'm not already counting down the days. 'Have you any plans?'

I plan to sleep in until eleven each day, read books about American teenagers living the sort of life I can only dream of, watch rubbish TV, eat a Snickers bar for breakfast and cheese on toast for lunch. When the sun is shining, I might venture out into the shared back garden and sit in the corner where we once had the trampoline, just to say I got some sun.

'Plans? Not really,' I say.

'Well, I have a task for you,' Mr Khan says. 'Let's call it a summer homework assignment. I want you to write me a list of five simple things you could do to build up your social life, both during and after the holiday. Just five. Can you do that, Eden?'

I go back to studying my shoes. Sometimes, Mr Khan seems to think I am about five years old.

I wish I was.

*

I'm sitting alone in the school canteen, picking little bits of sweetcorn out of my salad, when Chloe, Flick and Ima sit down next to me. They're nice girls, friendly girls – the kind of girl I used to be.

'Hey,' says Chloe. 'Looking forward to the holidays, Eden?'

I look up briefly though a curtain of fringe. 'Sure,' I say, dredging up a smile.

'Are you going to Lara's party?' Flick asks. 'Next Friday. It sounds amazing! Her brother's band are going to play and her parents are going out for the evening, so it will be like a proper grown-up party . . .'

'It'll be my first teen party ever,' Ima says, excitement fizzing behind her soft brown eyes. 'My parents are really strict, but we live quite close by so I'm allowed as long as I'm home by half ten. It's a bit of a sad curfew, but who cares? I'll take it! Come with us if you like, Eden. It'll be fun!'

I take a mouthful of quiche and chew slowly. Ima and the others are kind, but the truth is that Lara hasn't invited me to her party, even though I knew her well in primary school. She probably just assumed I wouldn't want to come, and I can't blame her for that. She assumed right.

'I'm busy that night,' I tell them. 'But yeah . . . it sounds good.'

Chatting with classmates about the holidays; would Mr Khan class that as building up my social life? Not when I am pretending to be busy on the night of a party, I suppose.

'Well,' Flick says, shrugging. 'If you do change your mind, let us know, OK?'

'Sure,' I say. 'Thanks. It's not that I don't want to come, just that I'm busy.'

We eat in awkward silence for a few minutes, and I feel a little bit bad about lying to them, pushing away their attempts at friendship. They're OK. They speak to me when lots of people don't bother, sit next to me occasionally at lunch or in the library. Sometimes, I partner Ima or Flick in PE. Maybe the four of us could be friends, if I was in the market for friendship, but I'm not.

Like I said, it's safer being alone. It hurts less.

Chloe looks at her mobile and pushes her plate away.

'Time to go,' she says. 'There's a meeting in the drama studio. Miss Gibson's running a youth drama group over the summer and we thought we might give it a try. Fancy coming along to find out more?'

'I can't,' I say carelessly, as if my lunchtimes are one long, hectic social whirl. 'Stuff to do in the library. Thanks, though. Have fun!'

Chloe, Flick and Ima gather up their bags and skitter away, waving over their shoulders.

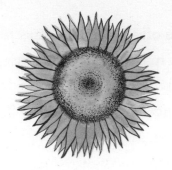

7

## Ryan

In Year Six, I'd have laughed at the idea that I might ever need counselling, that I'd one day be labelled as some kind of teenage troublemaker and not even care. I'd have hated the way some kids look at me wide-eyed and wary, as if I might randomly stab them with a biro or set fire to my backpack during assembly.

I'd have hated the way I've settled for friends like Buzz and Chris – boys who plan a career of trouble – who nick chocolate bars for fun and yell and swear in the street and kick empty Coke cans along the pavement just to scare old ladies and little kids. I am light entertainment, compared to them, but still I need Buzz and Chris. They are a distraction from the crackle of anger that fizzes just under my skin these days. They make me laugh at their clumsy, awkward antics, and I find myself drawn in, masterminding elaborate pranks, letting off steam in ill-advised blow-ups and scraps. Trouble and me are on first name terms, these days.

Sometimes I don't recognize the person I've become.

I had different plans for secondary school, once upon a time. I'd imagined I would have the best of all worlds; four cool girl mates and some boy mates too – the sporty, funny, easy-going kind rather than the ones I've ended up with. For ages the boys at primary school had teased me for hanging out with Andie, Eden, Tasha and Hasmita, but in the end they'd gone quiet with the jokes and wind-ups. They'd seemed almost envious, sometimes.

I'd been the kid who knew how to talk to girls, at a time when most of the other boys I knew were still telling fart jokes and scrapping in the playground to try to get the attention of the girls they liked. It didn't work, obviously, and slowly one or two were asking how come I got on so well with the Heart Club girls, how I knew what to talk about. I'd told them that there was no mystery, that you just talked about normal stuff and listened a bit and tried not to act like a total loser, but I'm not sure they believed me. Either way, I quite liked having their respect for a change.

I'd thought secondary school would be even better. My mates would be queuing up to ask for introductions to Andie, Tasha and Hasmita. I'd be the most popular boy in the school.

And maybe I'd be dating Eden by then . . . eventually, anyhow. Let's just say that by Year Six, I was nursing a serious crush.

In Year Six, Eden got sad. Her dad had left, taking a piece of her heart with him. It made me want to reach out and hold her hand, tell her I'd never leave her, but I didn't have the courage, of course.

Soon after there was an awkward phase when I'd realized that Andie was flirting with me. I didn't take much notice. I thought she was just practising for when she was going to break the heart of every boy at Moreton Park Academy, but there was more to it than that. Andie's crush was driving a wedge between her and Eden, but I tried not to worry too much. I pretended I hadn't noticed, waited for it to blow over. Soon everything would sort itself out. Secondary school would be a new chapter for all of us.

The new chapter had started a little sooner than we imagined, and not in the way I'd planned. One day towards the end of Year Six, Tasha came into school looking pink-eyed and shaky.

'Something terrible has happened!' she blurted, eyes brimming with tears. 'Something awful. It's the end of the world!'

Andie slid an arm around her. 'Hey, hey,' she said. 'Nothing can be that bad, Tash. Calm down; tell us what's up.'

Tasha bit her lip. 'My mum and dad,' she whispered. 'They have finally done it. They've ruined my life!'

Andie laughed. 'That's what parents do,' she said. 'They can't help it. It's a part of their job description. What's happened?'

Tasha just buried her face in her hands and howled, and nothing would console her. Her mum and dad were buying a house in France with a holiday cottage and a derelict barn attached. They were going to move there and rent the cottage out while they renovated the barn to turn it into more holiday lets.

'My dad's been made redundant,' Tasha said. 'He keeps

saying that it's a gift – that he can use his payout to start a whole new life. But what about my life? What about me?'

'It might be OK,' I said, half-heartedly. 'You might like it. And we could visit! I've never been to France.'

'Nor me,' Tasha wailed. 'And now I have to live there! I won't know anyone. I won't even be able to speak the language. And the place they've bought is in the middle of nowhere!'

'What are we going to do?' Hasmita wailed, an arm around Tasha's shoulder, brown eyes brimming with tears. 'You can't go to France, Tash! You're my best friend. It's a disaster!'

Andie sprang into action. 'It's not a disaster; it's an opportunity!' she announced. 'Just think, Tash, you'll get to live in a beautiful house in the country, in a place where it's sunny and warm! France is cool . . . they have sun-flowers growing all over the place, and artists wandering about, and they eat croissants for breakfast and cycle around in stripy tops with strings of onions around their necks! I've seen it in books.'

'I don't even like onions!' Tasha snuffled. 'And what about . . . what about us? The Heart Club?'

'Nothing will break us up,' Andie said firmly. 'Friends are forever.'

Tasha wasn't convinced.

'You lot will all be together,' she argued. 'And I will be stuck on my own, in some school where they do everything differently and they all speak French!'

'You'll soon learn,' Hasmita said, but she didn't look too sure.

'You'll make new friends, too,' Eden offered. 'French girls are probably really chic and cool. And I bet the boys are lush!'

'Almost as lush as me,' I quipped. 'Ooh la la!'

'It's not funny, Ryan!' Tasha huffed. 'I don't want to make new friends! I want you lot!'

'You've got us,' Andie said, firmly. 'Always, forever. Some things are unbreakable.'

But already, a little crack had zigzagged its way through the Heart Club, even if we didn't want to admit it.

8

# Eden

Chloe, Flick and Ima . . . they could be friends, maybe, if I let them. If I could only be brave and give them a chance, they'd let me tag along with them, include me in their plans. I wouldn't have to be on the edge of things any more.

Sometimes, I think I might like that.

Other times, I know they could never measure up to Andie, Tasha, Hasmita and Ryan, not in a million years. I lost my best friends once; I can't risk making new friends and losing them, too.

I was so lucky to have Andie, Ryan, Tash and Hasmita. I knew it even back then. A part of me had thought that maybe I didn't deserve them, that it couldn't really last forever.

'Idiot,' Andie used to say. 'Of course it can last. What could come between us? Nothing, Eden. Not ever. We're the Heart Club!'

I wanted to believe her, but the damage had already begun. Tasha's parents had signed the papers on the property in France and put their own house on the market. We weren't allowed to have sleepovers there any more, because everything had to stay ultra-tidy in case someone came to view the house.

Everything was changing. We were all best friends, sure, but just as Andie and I spent a lot of time together, Tasha and Hasmita did, too. Ryan, as always, drifted in and out of the group and spent time with his boy mates as well. Once Tasha was gone, how would we fit together?

Andie had always been the centre of our group, the glue that held us together. She was that kind of person – so sunny, so bright, so full of life. She made everything she touched seem cool. When you stood next to Andie, some of her sunshine spilled over on to you. That was a good feeling.

That was why I was so scared of losing her, because I

knew that without her I wouldn't be quite as cool, quite as fun, quite as real. I wouldn't be *me*.

I watched Andie to see if she was getting bored with me, if she found me less interesting, less exciting than she once had. I knew I wasn't as much fun as usual, now that Dad was gone. I was sad inside; what if Andie got fed up with that? I'd read in magazines that friendships changed as you got older, and old friends might suddenly outgrow each other. I didn't want to be the one left behind.

'What d'you think will happen when we go to secondary?' I'd asked, once. 'Will we still be close? People drift apart, don't they? Make new mates?'

Andie had grabbed my hands. 'Listen up, Eden Banks,' she'd said. 'You're my best friend, right? Always have been, always will be. We've been through loads together, bad stuff and good, and we'll go through loads more. We're going to go to uni together, right? I'll study art and you can do English or law or something brainy. We'll share a flat and have parties every single Saturday night.'

'And after uni we'll travel around the world together,' I'd chipped in, grinning. 'Hawaii, New York, Paris, Rome . . .'

'Exactly. And then we'll go to London and be rich and

famous, and one day we'll be bridesmaids at each other's weddings and our kids will be best mates, because we'll live just along the street from each other,' Andie'd concluded. 'So don't you even *think* that you can wriggle out of it, Eden. We're best friends forever, OK?'

She whirled me round and round until the two of us were so dizzy we fell over, laughing, and I forgot to be worried about secondary school. It seemed like the biggest leap, a jump into the unknown, but it didn't scare Andie, and if it didn't scare her then it didn't scare me.

'It'll be an adventure,' she'd promised. 'We're growing up, after all. It's time to move on. Moreton Park Academy sounds great! New subjects, new teachers, new challenges . . . it'll be awesome!'

I could almost believe it was true, as long as I didn't think too much about Tasha moving away. The ground that had felt so steady and solid under my feet all my life was shaky now, uncertain, liable to give way at any moment.

At the end of that last term at primary school, another disaster struck.

Hasmita announced that she wouldn't be going to Moreton Park Academy either.

'My parents want me to go to St Bernadette's,' she told us. 'I'm gutted. What am I going to do?'

St Bernadette's was a private girl's school in the next town. The girls had to wear bottle-green blazers with yellow piping and tartan kilts and tan tights with flat, lace-up shoes. They looked like something out of the 1930s.

Andie frowned. 'Can't you talk to your parents?' she asked Hasmita. 'Reason with them? They can't be serious!'

'They're serious all right,' Hasmita sighed. 'It's all arranged. I've tried to talk them round, but it's useless. It's not my fault I get good grades! They think that with a little bit of pushing I might turn out to be a doctor or a lawyer or a nuclear physicist, but I want to be a fashion stylist – they just won't listen! It's not just being separated from you lot. How am I going to learn to live with the ugliest school uniform in the northern hemisphere?'

'Those shoes,' I said. 'And tan tights!'

'That blazer,' Ryan chimed in.

'And no boys!' Tasha blinked. 'No boys at all!'

'Look on the bright side,' Andie said. 'No distractions. And I bet you can adapt the uniform. And we can still meet up on weekends . . .'

'Lucky thing,' Tasha said, with feeling.

'We're all lucky,' Andie insisted. 'We have each other. The Heart Club . . . no matter what.'

But the cracks were there, and they were spreading.

By the end of the summer the ground beneath my feet wasn't just shaky; a huge, gaping chasm had opened up, pulling everything I knew and loved down into its darkness.

9

## Ryan

Today, I am the only person in the entire school in lunch-time detention.

An outbreak of good behaviour in the run up to the end of term – who'd have thought it? All over school, kids must be handing in homework on time, being polite to teachers and fellow pupils.

Well, maybe. Buzz and Chris are still their usual wise-cracking, unpredictable selves and I don't suppose the bullies have stopped elbowing little kids in the ribs in order to nick their lunch money, or that the smokers have stopped gathering behind the school gym to cough their guts up. Moz Edwards was here at registration but missing from lessons, so I'm guessing the rates of truanting are pretty much the same as always.

Perhaps it's not so much that everyone is behaving perfectly, but more that the teachers have stopped caring as much.

I stroll over to the exclusion room, sending a gaggle of Year Seven girls into a frenzy of horrified whispers as I pass. I catch the words 'threatened an old lady with a spear' and turn round to pull a growly face at them, which sends them running along the corridor screeching. I try not to think too much about how it came to this, how I have turned into the sort of kid who terrifies Year Seven girls. I'm not proud of it.

Miss Robson looks as bored as I feel as she pretends to supervise the detention session, fiddling with her iPhone and watching the clock on the wall. Ten minutes before the end of lunch, her mobile trills with an incoming call; she glares at me before striding from the room, and I abandon today's punishment exercise, a short essay on the history of the javelin.

Very short, actually. It's not a subject I know very much about, in spite of the rumours.

Five minutes later, she's still not back, so I fold my essay into an origami paper crane, pocket it and leave the exclusion room. I'm just passing the library when I hear Miss Robson in the corridor ahead, still chatting on her mobile. Her boots make a clip-clop sound as she stalks towards me, but she's too busy with the call to notice me. I make a sharp left turn into the library and she goes clip-clopping past.

The librarian looks up, startled to see me. It's just minutes before the bell, and the place is busy. There are a couple of kids messing about on the computers, some Year Twelves revising, a few Year Sevens whispering in the magazine corner. My eyes come to rest on a lone dark-haired figure sitting at a table folding what looks like a tiny paper crane out of a chocolate bar wrapper. A Snickers bar, if I'm not mistaken.

Some things never change.

Eden Banks is not even on my radar these days – not usually – but here she is, twice in one day, pitching up right in my path. She looks sad, subdued, but of course that's nothing new.

We are different people from the Year Six kids who clowned around in the rain and kissed, awkwardly, in the porch of a half-flooded tent in Andie's garden. The whole world imploded after that, and we came out the other side a little bit broken, a little bit spoiled.

There is nothing to hold us together these days, but my eyes latch on to the tiny chocolate wrapper paper crane, and I smile in spite of myself.

Eden looks up at me through her dipping fringe, and two spots of pink appear on her cheeks, as if making paper cranes is something childish, foolish — something to be ashamed of. I want to tell her that it isn't.

'You still remember how to make them, then?' I ask.

'Yeah, of course! How could I forget?'

Then the bell goes, and the library kids jump up and into action, hauling on rucksacks, gathering folders, stampeding for the doors. In the chaos, I take the detention paper crane from my pocket and put it on the desk in front of Eden.

I look back over my shoulder as I head for the door, and she's smiling.

10

## Eden

I'm walking out of school at the end of the day when a girl running the wrong way along the corridor crashes into me and drops her shoulder bag on the floor. Books, pens and bits of paper spill out in all directions, and we both dip down to pick up the spills.

'Eden!' the girl says, and I look up through my fringe and realize it's Lara, the party girl Chloe, Flick and Ima were talking about earlier. 'I'm sorry . . . wasn't looking where I was going!'

I smile weakly and hand her a couple of exercise books and a loose-leaf folder that has skidded under a radiator.

'How's it going?' she asks, as if she hasn't seen me at all

in the last two years. She probably hasn't; I am all but invisible lately. 'All good?'

'Yeah, all good,' I mutter, scooping up a handful of small card tickets that are scattered around us. They are invites for next week's party, which is slightly awkward, but I shuffle them together like they're playing cards and push them at her, pretending I haven't noticed.

'Oh yeah . . . the party . . .' she says, pulling a face. 'Are you coming? I'd love it if you did, Eden. I mean, we don't see much of each other now, but we used to get on well, didn't we? In the old days . . . So come if you can, for old times' sake. Bring some friends!'

She hands me an invitation, then gathers up her bag and skips past me along the corridor.

Looks like I have an invitation to the party of the year.

I used to like parties, once.

The Heart Club did the best parties ever, sleepover parties, picnic parties, camp-out parties, Christmas parties where we gave ourselves sugar highs eating home-made yule log and hot chocolate with cream and marshmallows. We never got to have a grown-up party, though, unless you count the farewell party Tasha's parents had thrown a few weeks before they left for France.

The party had been just a few days before our ill-fated garden camp-out and Tasha's dad had already taken a vanload of stuff to the new house by then, so their place was looking a bit bare. The new people were moving in three weeks later, but Tasha's mum reckoned they'd probably need that long to clear everything up after the party. 'Let's make it a good one,' she'd said.

Everyone was there – me, Andie, Ryan, Hasmita and our families too, along with all kinds of other people Tasha's family were friendly with. It was the first time the Heart Club had partied with all five families in attendance, though. Me and Mum had baked a cake for Tasha's family and iced it in the colours of the French flag, and it made Tasha's mum cry; she said she'd never seen anything so lovely.

'She's been drinking wine,' Tasha whispered to me. 'She's tipsy, and Dad's worse – he's started speaking with a cheesy French accent and kissing everyone on both cheeks. He thinks it's funny. I am so embarrassed!'

'Don't be,' Andie told her. 'It's cute. All parents are

embarrassing; it's what they do best – they can't help it, really!'

It turned out that Andie was right. All the grown-ups drank too much wine and danced badly to dodgy 1980s pop and got too loud or too emotional or too nostalgic, or sometimes all three. Andie's parents were trying to do the salsa on the lawn and somehow got tangled up in the washing line, and Ryan's parents tried to untangle them and managed to pull the whole thing down, along with a string of fairy lights.

'We'll never be like them,' Hasmita said as she watched her mum leading a flash mob dance to something painful called 'The Birdie Song', which can't have been easy in a sari. 'We'll be cool and wild and awesome, not dodgy. Right?'

'I might be a bit dodgy,' Ryan confessed.

'No "might" about it,' I'd teased, then felt my ears go pink as he gave me one of his big lopsided grins.

Tasha was grinning too, but her cheeks were wet with tears.

'I am going to miss you guys so, so much,' she said. 'I'll never forget you, not ever. I promise!'

I believed her at the time, but then I believed a lot of things back then. Promises – they're more easily broken than you think.

I emailed Tasha a few times after the move, but I never once heard back. I don't exactly blame her, because things had got so crazy by then that I wished I could run away from it, too. I'd have gone to a desert island and never come back, or turned hermit and hidden away in a cave in a forest with just birds and mice for company.

I wanted the world to go away, but still, I was missing Tasha. She was one of the few people I knew who might understand, even if she was miles away in France.

edenb@zippmail.com
to tashatoocool@moremail.co.uk

I think this week has been the hardest week of my whole life. I can't make sense of any of it, and I can't believe you've gone to France – I keep thinking that if I walk down to Baskerville Avenue you'll be there, the same as always. You're not, though. You're hundreds of miles away in France, just when I need you most. It can't be easy for you either, Tash – are you OK? Are you coping? What's

the new house like? Please ask your mum to give in and buy you a mobile, because then we could actually text and phone. Miss you like mad.
Eden xxx

edenb@zippmail.com
to tashatoocool@morcmail.co.uk

I expect you've been very busy with the move and everything, and Mum says you might not even have the Internet connected yet, but please, please reply, Tash. I really, really need someone to talk to, someone away from all this mess. School starts tomorrow and I am dreading it. Please reply, Tash. Missing you. Eden xxx

edenb@zippmail.com
to tashatoocool@moremail.co.uk

It's been six weeks, Tasha, and not a word. School sucks big time, in case you're wondering. I don't suppose you are. I guess you've moved on, made a fresh start, left the past behind. I wish I could do that. I don't blame you and I wish you well, but don't worry – I get the message. I won't be emailing again. Eden xxx

I didn't think anything could make me hurt more than I was already hurting, but I was wrong. I'd lost Andie, I'd lost Ryan, I'd lost Hasmita and Tasha. Friends fell through my fingers like sand, the summer after Year Six, until one by one they were all gone.

# 11

## Ryan

I slip my key into the lock on Thursday evening, home from playing footy in the park with Buzz, Chris and the others, and step into a nightmare. Mr Khan is sitting right there in my living room, sipping tea and talking to Mum and Dad.

Anger floods my body, hot and dangerous. Mum and Dad must have known about this, surely? Teachers don't just turn up at your house at random to dunk chocolate chip biscuits and discuss the weather. It's a set-up.

'Ah, Ryan,' Mr Khan says. 'You're back! I just popped over to have a chat with your parents, make sure we're all on the same page with this . . .'

I clench my fists. 'Get out,' I say in a small voice. 'Please. I can't do this; I don't want you here!'

Mum is on her feet, face anxious. 'Ryan, Mr Khan is worried about you – we all are! The incident with the javelin . . . well, I don't think we realized just how angry you were feeling. Apparently there's a special kind of counselling you can do to help you manage your moods . . .'

'Anger management,' Mr Khan says. 'We discussed it last session, didn't we, Ryan?'

I take in a ragged breath. 'I don't need anger management,' I say gruffly. 'I just need people to stop bugging me. Like you, Mr Khan, and your stupid, do-gooding plans to turn me into a model citizen. Just go, OK? Get out of my house!'

'Ryan!' Dad says. 'Watch your manners! Mr Khan is trying to help you. God knows, we've done our best, but this latest thing – attacking old ladies – it's too much. I'm at the end of my tether, son. This temper of yours . . . unless you sort it out, it's going to land you in big trouble!'

Dad's words are like a knife in my gut, but it's Mum who really twists that knife.

'The school is trying to help you, Ryan,' she says, her

eyes brimming with tears. 'We're trying to help you, but you won't let us! Why do you push everyone away? Why can't you just be the way you used to be?'

Why can't I be the way I used to be? I can't, I can't, I can't. Why don't they understand?

Rocket pushes his damp nose against my hand, whimpering, and suddenly the fight goes out of me. What's the point in kicking the furniture, punching a wall, shouting and swearing at the injustice of it all? That will only upset Mum and Dad more.

Self-loathing floods me and I sink to my knees, put my arms round Rocket, kid myself that he understands. What's wrong with me? Why can't I get my act together? Why does every single thing I do go so badly wrong?

Mr Khan approaches gingerly, leans down to put a hand on my shoulder. I want to shake him off, but I take a deep breath and bury my face in Rocket's fur, and I manage to endure it.

'It doesn't have to be this way,' Mr Khan says. 'All this anger. We can help you get to the bottom of it, find safer ways to express your feelings. We can help you, I promise.'

'I don't want to talk to you,' I grind out. 'I can't, OK?'

'Fine,' Mr Khan says, seemingly unconcerned. 'We're probably not the greatest match, therapy-wise. I can find you somebody you feel more comfortable with, Ryan; someone you can talk to. Will you think about it?'

I say nothing, and that silence takes all the strength and courage I have. Mr Khan retreats. I hear my parents ushering him to the door, apologizing over and over.

I head to my room and fling myself on the bed, fists clenched.

I don't need anyone's help. I'll show them.

## 12

## **Eden**

After school, I head into town to swap my library books, picking out three new titles to start the holidays with. There is only one more day of lessons and I seriously cannot wait because school is a total waste of time right now. The teachers have switched off, dreaming of sunny holidays in Corfu or Gran Canaria, keeping order in class (almost) by handing out quizzes, word searches and sweets.

I'm looking forward to some lazy days and long lie-ins, but a part of me can't help remembering the way summers used to be, back in the Heart Club days. We'd spend ages making plans . . . organizing picnics, bike rides, sleepovers, projects. Once we made cupcakes and gave them away to random people in the park. Once, when Andie was having a vegetarian phase, we dressed up in animal onesies and handed out home-made flyers about endangered species in the street.

Summers always used to be so busy, so much fun. I miss those days.

I'm walking towards the railway station with my armful of books when three girls in St Bernadette's uniform come out and start heading towards me. I always panic when I see that uniform – the distinctive green blazers with gold trim, the knee-length tartan skirts – but the truth is I hardly ever bump into Hasmita now. Her mum drives her in most days, I think, but today I am unlucky because the girl in the middle, laughing with her friends, is unmistakable.

Her long dark hair is parted into two neat fishtail plaits, and her dark eyes are shining. My heart lurches. I'd run away, cross the road, turn round and walk the other way, but it's too late.

Hasmita looks at me, and I watch the smile slide off her face.

They're walking towards me, closer and closer, and I'm unable to summon a smile, a word. What has happened to me? How can I let the girl who was once one of my best friends just walk past?

I peer out through my fringe, twist my mouth into something that's almost a grin.

'Hello, Hasmita,' I say, but my voice sounds gritty, dry, like sand and ashes.

Hasmita's eyes widen, horrified, and then she's past me, gone.

'Who was *that?*' one of her friends asks.

'Nobody,' Hasmita says. 'Just some girl I used to know.'

It's like a slap.

I keep walking, head down, cheeks flaming. I am a nobody, a girl whose old friends pretend they never knew her. My breath feels jagged, painful, and my heart aches for what has been lost. What would Andie have said if she could see the way we've fallen apart? She'd have known what to do, how to fix things, but Andie's not around any more. She can't help. I wish she could.

I tilt my chin and adjust my route home to take a trip down memory lane, walking along Castle Street, Andie's old street, once as familiar as my own.

These are the pavements we raced our scooters along,

the doors we knocked on patiently hoping to sell hand-drawn programmes for a circus extravaganza we planned to put on in Andie's back garden. We only sold one, and that was to Ryan's mum, who probably just felt sorry for us. We were six years old, full of hopes and dreams and impossible plans that seemed entirely possible at the time. In the end, the show was cancelled because we couldn't get Andie's cat to jump through a hoop, or perfect our cartwheels, or learn how to tightrope walk on the washing line or turn Andie's swing into a trapeze.

Six years old. We had no clue, back then, how things would turn out. I guess that was just as well.

I turn the corner and my heart lurches as I catch sight of two small girls sitting on the low wall in front of Andie's house. Just for a moment, it feels like I've stepped back into my own memories, but of course a new family live in Andie's old house now, a family with small children. As I draw nearer I can see that the two little girls are selling lemonade in paper cups for 20p a shot; they've painted a sign that flutters in the breeze, anchored to the wall by two stones.

We made lemonade too, once, Andie and me, but it was

at my house, not here. We squeezed lemons and boiled up water with sugar and stirred everything together. Mum showed us how to smoosh up a bowlful of strawberries to make the lemonade pink, and although we were disappointed that it wasn't fizzy, it tasted great once it was cooled and served with lots of ice.

The lemonade on offer here is the shop-bought kind; I can see a plastic bottle partly concealed in a flower bed.

'It's for charity,' the older girl calls out as I try to mooch past. 'Probably. The dogs' home, or maybe orphans or something.'

'Or sweets,' the younger one pipes up, and her sister jabs her swiftly with an elbow.

'Please buy one,' she implores. 'For the sake of those poor, orphaned . . . um . . . dogs!'

I roll my eyes and fish 20p from a pocket.

'Only 10p extra for pink lemonade!' she declares, unleashing a syrupy dribble of red food colouring into one of the drinks and stirring it briskly with a teaspoon. 'Specially for you!'

Grudgingly, I find an extra coin and exchange it for the lemonade, which now looks like a cross between fizzing tomato soup and something a vampire might drink. Still, they're only kids.

'Lovely,' I say. 'Good luck with your fund-raising!'

As I walk away, I hear them giggling.

'If they're all as stupid as she is,' the older girl says, 'We'll make a fortune!'

I tip my lemonade into the gutter and stuff the paper cup into the litter bin on the corner, then head for home.

## 13

# Ryan

It's the last day of school, but I seriously do not need another day of detentions. What I do need is to clear my name, to show Mum and Dad I am not someone who terrorizes old ladies for fun. Anger management? No thanks. Counselling? Not a chance. I don't need a bunch of shrinks on my case. I've got by without all that for two years, and I plan on keeping things that way.

I give school a swerve and head to the garden centre. This is not my natural habitat, and it costs me an unbelievable £20 of my savings to buy the supplies I need. A few poxy plants – who knew they could cost so much?

I trudge towards school carrying boxes of greenery;

walking past the school gates and round the corner gives me great pleasure. I know exactly which house I'm looking for . . . Miss Smith lives in number forty-one, a 1930s semi with peeling paintwork and an overgrown garden. If I'd been unsure, the newly built fence would have given it away; the school's solution to the hazard of low-flying javelins. It looks stark and ugly, badly constructed from rough orange planks.

I glance towards the house, but there's no sign of life. I don't want to get caught poking around in Miss Smith's garden, even though I'm planning to fix it up a bit. Knowing my luck, I'd be accused of vandalism. Luckily, the coast is clear.

I push open the rickety gate. The pond where the javelin landed is silted up with reeds and duckweed, an empty beer can floating where once goldfish might have swum. There's an ugly old dead tree in the middle of the grass – no leaves, no buds, nothing. It's like a giant bunch of jaggedy twigs sticking up out of the ground, with an empty, rusted bird feeder swinging from one branch, squeaking slightly in the breeze. The whole place is a mess, with nettles and brambles where the flower beds should be and dandelions sprouting between the paving stones. The grass is knee high and there are Coke cans and crisp packets everywhere, blown in from the street.

Miss Smith is probably too old to do much gardening, but I can see she might have liked all that stuff once. There are straggly old rose bushes in among the nettles and a couple of shrubs that have turned triffid and tried to take over.

I'm not sure where to start, but clearing the nettles and brambles seems the logical place. I pull out an old trowel I've found and start work. It takes longer than I imagine – every time I get one corner tidy, I spot something else that needs sorting, but the work is strangely calming. It reminds me of long ago, learning to grow beans and sunflowers in Gran and Grandad's garden.

An hour in, I think I see curtains twitch in the house, but no outraged old lady appears, so I decide I'm probably imagining it.

At one point, the woman from next door wanders out and pauses at the gate to watch me filling the wheelie bin with litter, nettles and brambles.

'Who are you, then?' she asks with a frown. 'Did the

community council send you? Because that garden is a bloomin' disgrace. An eyesore, it is.'

'I'm a family friend,' I say.

'Oh?' the woman says, sceptical. 'Didn't know she had any family, being a spinster and all that. There is a nephew somewhere, but he never bothers himself. Poor old dear shouldn't be living on her own at her age. Did you hear about those louts from the school, threatening her with javelins?'

'No,' I say shortly. 'I didn't.'

'Well, they did,' she informs me. 'Hooligans, the lot of them. Kids today; no discipline! Who did you say you were again? Shouldn't *you* be at school?'

'My school broke up last week,' I lie.

'Hmmph. Well, it's high time someone gave the old dear a hand with that garden. Like a jungle, it is. You'd think one of the neighbours would lend a hand . . .'

'*You're* one of the neighbours,' I point out.

'Well, yes,' she admits. 'But I've got a bad back. And Miss Smith isn't what you'd call friendly; thinks she's too good for the likes of me, she does. And lately she's gone a bit doolally. Alzheimer's, I expect. She wants putting in one of those homes, if you ask me.'

88

I grit my teeth. 'Nobody did ask you,' I snap. 'Luckily.'

The woman pulls an outraged face and bustles off next door again, and I get planting. I shove in loads of little purple and yellow flowers that look like they have smiley faces and a couple of clumps of flashy daisy-type things. I dig a big hole next to the ugly orange fence and plant a climber that the man in the garden centre said was as tough as old boots, guaranteed to scramble all over a fence and flower like crazy. I am just brushing down my jeans when the back door of the house creaks open.

Miss Smith is there, leaning on a metal walking stick, clutching a chipped blue mug. Embarrassment washes over me like a wave; the only thing worse than chucking an accidental javelin into her garden is being caught in the act of trying to put things right. My bad boy image is slipping.

I walk towards her, planning an apology and a hasty retreat, but her face is all smiles and wrinkles. She looks about a hundred and three, seriously.

'Peter?' she says, her voice all wispy like dry leaves in winter. 'I made you hot chocolate. Your favourite!'

She thinks I am someone else. Someone helpful and

heroic, perhaps a long-lost relative or a do-gooding neighbour from years gone by. Someone who likes hot chocolate
and weeding, not a juvenile delinquent, a javelin-wielding
maniac. It's probably just as well.

I take the mug, but it's empty except for an old teabag
and a few dregs of cold tea. I don't care – it's not exactly
hot chocolate weather, anyhow.

'Sorry about the javelin,' I say, but Miss Smith's eyes are
glassy and distant and I don't think she's listening. 'It wasn't
deliberate . . .'

'Come again soon, Peter,' she says. 'It's been so very long
since I've seen you. I'll make an apple pie next time!'

'Thing is, I'm not actually Peter,' I say. 'I'm Ryan.'

'You're a good boy,' she says, patting my arm with a
claw-like hand. 'Goodbye, Peter!'

I pick up my rucksack and head off, smiling all the
way home.

# 14

## Eden

'Beautiful day out there,' Mum announces brightly, appearing in the bedroom doorway like a messenger of doom. 'Any plans, Eden?'

It feels more like the middle of the night, but I groan and peer blearily over the duvet.

'My plans are to sleep,' I mutter. 'It's the holidays, remember?'

'You had a lie-in on Saturday,' she points out. 'And Sunday. And Monday. Wake up, Eden! Stop letting life pass you by!' She drags the curtains open abruptly and the room floods with sunlight, sending me scrabbling beneath the covers.

'Noooooooo! What are you *doing?*'

The duvet is dragged firmly from my hands, and I surface to find Mum sitting on the windowsill, her face determined. I know when I am beaten. I sit up, scowling.

'I need you to do an errand for me,' Mum is saying. 'It's my friend Jo's birthday on Friday and I've ordered her one of those gorgeous coffee-table cookery books, all healthy stuff and juices and cake made out of chia seeds. She'll love it. I need you to pick it up from the bookshop for me.'

'Why can't you just pick it up after work?' I grumble.

'I'm working late all week,' she says briskly. 'Come on, love, it's not much to ask!'

'But, Mum . . . I don't want to go to town!' I argue. 'I've got tons of studying to do this holiday!'

'Looks like it,' she says, raising a sceptical eyebrow. 'Look. You're a clever girl, Eden, you'll find the time. I won't get a chance to pick it up myself. Jo's my best friend, and it's her birthday. Be fair . . . I don't often ask you to do this kind of thing, do I?'

'Suppose not,' I admit.

'Good. That's sorted, then. Maybe we could try a few of the recipes ourselves; you used to like that kind of thing. Cakes and baking . . .'

I roll my eyes. 'When I was a kid,' I say, scornfully. 'Not now.'

Mum's shoulders slump. 'Well, whatever. Pick up the book – I've left a note of the title and author on the table downstairs, along with some cash. Can you go to Tesco Metro and pick up a few bits and pieces to eat, too? I'm covering late shifts all week, and on Friday I'll be going straight from work to meet Jo for a birthday drink, so you're going to have to fix your own meals. I'm sorry; it's all a bit rubbish, really. But if you could do a little shop and then maybe meet up with a friend for a milkshake or a coffee, whatever . . .'

I grit my teeth.

'Mum,' I cut in. 'I'll do your errands, fine, but please stay out of my social life! I don't need your help!'

'OK, OK, I just thought . . . well, it might be nice to meet up with some friends while you're out.'

'Mum!'

She jumps up from the windowsill, miming a sad, can't-blame-me-for-trying expression. 'I won't be in until past seven,' she says. 'Thanks a million, pet . . . and see you later!'

Moments later I hear the door click shut and I am finally left in peace. It's no use though. I can't get back to sleep. Ridiculously, my mobile says it's just past eight o'clock.

I shower, dress and eat a lazy breakfast, but already I am dreading the trip to town. Mum is only trying to help, I know, but there is no way I want to 'meet up with friends' for a milkshake. There are no friends to meet up with any more; she knows that, surely?

Maybe she's been chatting with Mr Khan, plotting ways to give me a personality transplant.

I am usually meticulous about homework, but Mr Khan's assignment is just fluffy pseudo psychology. Why take it seriously? Against my better judgement, I take out my note-book and write a title in fancy lettering: Ways To Improve My Pitiful Social Life. I begin to write.

1. Be sure to smile brightly at everyone and make cheery small talk at every opportunity.
2. Join an after-school club. Perhaps stamp-collecting, or crochet?
3. Suggest jolly outings to bond with classmates. Bike rides, picnics, trips to the seaside?

4. Always look on the bright side. A sunny personality wins friends.
5. Accept all party invitations with enthusiasm. Dress prettily and be charming to all.

This exercise in sarcasm doesn't hold my attention for long, and at eleven o'clock I take a deep breath and head for town. I don't want to run the risk of bumping into someone from school on the bus, so I walk in, skulking along in Converse, baggy grey jeans and a black hoodie, my eyes outlined with thick black kohl. At home, the mirror tells me I look good – bold and brave and confident. Outside, I catch glimpses of my reflection as I pass the shiny plate-glass shop windows, and realize I just look sad and lost.

I tilt my chin high and pretend not to care. Collecting the book is easy, and I head on to Tesco to buy pizza, oven chips, coleslaw, quiche. I browse the High Street for a while. The little paper crane Ryan gave me is in my hoodie pocket for luck, and on impulse I treat myself to some patterned paper to make some origami cranes of my own. I'm just heading home when I spot Chloe, Flick and Ima further along the pavement.

Great.

Instinctively I put my head down and act like I haven't noticed them, but it's too late – Ima is calling my name. They come towards me, all grins and whoops, and I look up through my fringe and pretend I'm happy to see them.

'Hey!' Chloe says. 'Great to see you! We've been shopping . . . well, window shopping, anyway!'

'Cool,' I say. 'I've just been . . . doing stuff.'

I think my mouth is malfunctioning. It's coming out with rubbish, but Chloe, Flick and Ima don't seem to notice.

'Everyone's in town today,' Ima is saying. 'It's crazy! Summer holiday madness. Anyhow, we're just going to Costa to get frappés . . . there's a whole bunch of Year Nine boys in there. Want to come?'

'No, no; I can't,' I bluster, panicked. 'I'm in a hurry. Doing . . . things.'

'Whatever,' Flick shrugs. 'See you at Lara's party, then?'

'Yeah, yeah, definitely,' I bluff, and they're on their way, giggling, chatting, waving goodbye.

I take in a ragged breath as if I've just been through some kind of trauma. If losing the power of coherent speech counts as a trauma, I probably have. I think of my five-point plan to improve my social life, of Mum's suggestion that I meet some friends for a milkshake, and I want to cry.

It won't happen, because I do not want a social life. I do not want friends.

It hurts too much when they go away.

I square my shoulders and walk on, and that's when I see her.

She's standing outside Topshop, just across the road, looking at her mobile phone. She is taller than when I last saw her and much more grown-up – her face has lost that round, pink-cheeked, childish look. Her hair is still long and ash blonde, hanging over one shoulder in a neat pony-tail, and her pale lashes are dark with mascara. She's wearing a cute little print dress, a cardi and lace-up ankle boots with a tiny heel, which don't seem like her style at all . . . but still, it's her all right.

I'd know Andie Carson anywhere.

## 15

## Ryan

When my head fills up with thoughts I don't want to think, I run away. I don't pack a rucksack or leave a goodbye note, because it's not that kind of running away, and I don't go far or stay away for long. It's a coward's kind of running, I suppose, and it can only ever work for a little while, because the things I am running from are with me the whole time. They're inside my head.

Today I wake up angry, which happens quite a lot.

I've been thinking of Mum and Dad and how disappointed they are in me. I've been thinking of Mr Khan and how he thinks it's somehow OK to turn up in my living room, discussing shrinks and counselling with my family. Most of all, though, I've been thinking of Miss Smith and the over-grown garden, now a little tidier and planted up with cheap bedding plants. I think of her bird feeder, swinging empty from the fossilized tree, and the way she thought my name was Peter and tried to give me hot chocolate, but couldn't quite remember how. Where is the real Peter? Where are her family, her friends? How come a delinquent kid has to do her weeding and chop down the brambles? Old age sucks.

Actually, life sucks, full stop.

If you think about these things too much, they make you sad, and that's bad news. I've seen what sad has done to Eden Banks, how it snuffed out the light in her eyes, leached the colour right out of her life. Sad is not for me.

Angry is better than sad, but still, it gets into your blood. It fizzes through you like a virus, seeping into everything. It makes you kick chairs, throw school books into waste-paper bins, javelins into gardens. It makes you sneer at teachers, cheek your parents, punch a wall, push the bound-aries. Even your friends treat you carefully, like you're a firework that might suddenly go off in their face. Not that I have friends any more, not really . . . Buzz and Chris are more partners in crime.

The truth is that anger gets you into a whole lot of trouble, so I run, and that takes the edge off things a little.

I don't make a fuss about it. I run in jeans and T-shirt, with a hoody I can take off when I get too warm. I have good trainers, the kind that let me run on pavements or fields, through rain, slush, snow, fallen leaves, zombie apocalypse.

Well, you get the idea.

I also have Rocket, my dog, who never wakes up angry but is always full of joy. When I run with him the joy rubs off on me a little, eventually, just for a while. I think life must be much easier for dogs. No school, no chores, no regrets. Usually we run early in the morning or late at night, because those times are quiet, but right now I head out in broad daylight because I want to outrun the bad thoughts in my head and I don't much care who sees me.

We run along the edge of the woods, towards town, towards the park. I settle into an easy, loping pace, my feet slapping the pavement, my breath fast and easy. I can feel my muscles stretching, feel the anger slowly seeping away. Every bit of me feels alive. Rocket runs beside me, bright-eyed, happy. His tail waves like a flag.

I will keep running until the anger has gone, make maybe one or two circuits of the park. Then I'll throw sticks for Rocket, and maybe buy an ice cream.

16

## Eden

My eyes open wide and my heart constricts with shock. As I try to make sense of it, Andie looks up, eyes sparkling, her face lighting up with that big trademark grin that has been melting my heart since forever. Today, though, it leaves me numb, speechless.

'Eden!' she calls. 'Hey! I've been waiting for you! Long time no see!'

A sick, sour feeling pools in my belly and I turn and shove my way through the crowded street of shoppers, away from Andie. She can't be here, surely? And why on earth would she be waiting for me?

'Eden, wait up!'

She falls into step beside me, half-running; puts a hand on my arm, squeezes gently.

'Slow down, Eden, please.' she says. 'Don't run away from me. I know it's been ages, I know I should have been in touch . . .'

I shrug off her touch, my heart pounding. My eyes are blurry but I don't cry any more; I tilt my chin upwards and stride along, hoping she'll get sick of following. She doesn't.

'Look, I'm sorry, OK?' Andie tells me. 'Listen to me, Eden! I'm sorry, I'm sorry, I'm sorry! I've let you down, I should have been in touch . . . but I was angry. It was a mess, OK? Can we talk? Please?'

'I don't even know why you're here!' I snap.

'I'm here to make things right,' she says. 'Everything went wrong, and we all blamed each other, and look at the mess we're in now! Come on, Eden, I've come all this way to see you . . . surely you can spare half an hour to talk to me? Please? For old times' sake?'

I look at Andie and the fight goes out of me. My shoulders slump.

'Shall we go to the park?' she suggests. 'Like we used to?'

We walk across town to the park, slip through the gates and into the greenery.

'Tell me why you're here,' I ask again, and she explains that she's down until the weekend – a family visit, the first one since the move to Scotland.

'I just want to spend some time with you,' she explains. 'It ended badly, didn't it? We were supposed to be friends forever, but we messed up, and it plays on my mind, Eden. I can't move on . . . I feel bad. Can't we sort things out, clear the air?'

'It's too late,' I say. 'Some things can't be fixed.'

'But we can,' Andie says. 'We're different! We had – have – something special! Hey, shall we go to the swings?'

She drags me over to the children's playground, scene of a million childhood memories. We perch awkwardly alongside each other on the swings, creaking listlessly back and forth.

'You've changed, you know,' she says, as if it might have escaped my attention. 'I almost didn't recognize you. Your hair . . . it's so different . . . so dramatic. And your clothes. You used to wear bright colours, so all that black is a bit of a shock. Goth-chic, right? And you seem . . . I don't know.

Maybe I've got this all wrong, but you seem kind of subdued. Kind of sad.'

'I'm fine,' I growl. 'Is this why you're here, Andie? Are you going to pick us apart, one at a time? Tell me I'm sad? Tell Ryan he's angry and out of control? I never see Hasmita any more, but I expect you'll find some insult for her, too, and Tasha . . .'

'That's not what this is about.' Andie frowns. 'I've missed you, Eden, can't you see that? You were my best friend, and I left without explaining things, without saying goodbye.'

I scuff my feet across the soft surface of the playground.

'I don't have time to see Ryan and Hasmita, and obviously, Tasha's moved away . . .' She trails off into silence, looking guilty. 'Look, d'you want the truth? I don't think I can face them, Eden, not right now. Much as I love them, it's you I've come to see. So don't tell them you've seen me, OK? I don't want them to feel bad.'

I almost laugh. There is exactly zero chance of me telling Ryan, Hasmita or Tasha that I've seen Andie, because I won't be seeing them either.

'I just have some loose ends to tie up,' Andie is saying. 'This is about us two, Eden. About our friendship . . .'

'Do we have a friendship?' I ask.

'You know we do!'

Andie is silent, swinging slowly back and forth for a while. Abruptly she jumps off the swing and turns to face me. Her fingers fidget with the neckline of her little print dress. There's a glint of silver in the spring sunshine as she tugs a pendant out into the light, a small broken-heart pendant on a slender chain.

'Remember this?' she asks. 'You bought it for me on my eleventh birthday. A best friends necklace . . . I still wear it, Eden. Do you wear yours?'

I nod wordlessly. My fingers tremble as they scoop out a matching silver chain, the other half of the broken-heart pendant. I've worn it all this time, just like Andie.

'Best friends, Eden,' she says. 'It ended badly, like I said, but I haven't stopped thinking about you, not ever. I'm here because I want to repair the friendship, make things right again. Please tell me I'm not too late.'

I shake my head, hardly daring to believe it.

'Not too late,' I whisper. 'Oh, Andie!'

Suddenly we're hugging – awkward, anxious, holding on as if we'll never let go. I want to laugh and cry all at once, because Andie still smells of the same vanilla shower gel she always loved. It's like someone has reached out and wiped away the last two years, erased everything bad that ever happened.

'Friends forever,' Andie says, and her breath smells of toothpaste against my cheek and she holds me so tight it's as if she's trying to anchor me. I'm not sure who is holding who, which one of us needs to be anchored – and I don't even care.

We have so much to catch up on, and we've barely even scratched the surface when the cheesy jingle of the ice-cream van drifts through the air. It's the exact same jingle as always, and Andie's face lights up the way it always did.

'Want one?' I ask. 'Wait there . . . I'll treat you!'

I join the queue at the ice-cream van and order two 99s with strawberry sauce, Andie's favourite. As I turn to head back to the playground, though, I frown. There's nobody around except for a couple of mums with toddlers and little kids, fooling around on the seesaw and the roundabout.

The swings are empty, swaying a little in the spring sunshine.

## 17

## **Ryan**

After two circuits of the park I'm on top of the world. The anger is long gone, replaced by a euphoria that only ever comes from running. I feel the way I used to feel before everything turned to dust in my hands.

I throw sticks for Rocket and he finds a tennis ball in the bushes and we play footy with that for a while, and then I hear the chimes of the ice-cream van on the other side of the park and decide to treat myself.

I don't actually get there though, because standing on the path just next to the playground is Eden Banks, holding two ice-cream cones that are dripping on to her hands.

'Lost someone?' I wisecrack. 'Or did you just count wrong? I thought you were good at maths?'

'Yes. No . . .' Her cheeks flame pink and she looks around her, as if the owner of the extra 99 ice-cream cone might be watching from behind a tree or hiding behind the ladder of the playground slide.

'I thought I saw someone I knew,' she explains, frowning. 'Looks like they've gone, though. D'you want an ice cream? Free to a good home?'

'Happy to help out,' I say, taking the offered ice cream carefully.

We stand in silence for a while, tidying up the drips, biting into the chocolate flakes. Eden looks brighter, happier than I have seen her in a while.

'Still the best ice cream in the world,' I say. 'Ages since I've had a 99.'

Rocket nudges Eden with his nose, hoping for ice cream, and she laughs. I haven't heard that laugh in a very long time.

'Rocket, no!' I scold. 'Just ignore him. He'd do anything for ice cream. A bit like me . . .'

She bites her lip. 'You have a dog called Rocket,' she says. 'Really? Finally?'

When we were kids I used to ask for a dog every birthday and Christmas.

'A dog is for life, not just for Christmas,' Andie always teased me, parroting some advert she'd seen about unwanted pets, and I'd set out to prove that my imaginary dog would be the most loved mutt in the world. I used to draw endless pictures of the dog at school, an untidy, dishevelled black and white mongrel. I named my imaginary companion Rocket.

'He'll be the fastest dog you ever saw,' I told the others. 'And the naughtiest!'

'So is he?' Eden is asking now. 'Is he the fastest dog in the world?'

'Just the naughtiest,' I admit, and Rocket pushes his head against Eden's leg, content, asking to be petted.

'You've made a new friend,' I say.

'I never thought your parents would cave in,' she whispers, ducking down to stroke Rocket. 'They were always so against it! How did you persuade them?'

'They changed,' I shrug. 'I've changed. You've changed. It happens.'

She raises an eyebrow. 'Really? Who knew?'

I see a trace of the girl I used to know back in the old days, before the Heart Club fell to pieces and us along with it. She feeds Rocket the last of her ice-cream cone, and he guzzles it and rolls over to have his tummy scratched, like she's his new best friend.

We never talk any more, Eden and I, but we have so much shared history. Paper cranes, 99s with strawberry sauce and so much more.

'Have you ever thought of letting your hair go back to its natural colour?' I ask, and Eden's face shuts down, closes off.

'Have you ever thought of minding your own business?'

'It was just an idea. I liked it that way.'

'I didn't.'

She's walking away from me now, and I run alongside her, Rocket galloping on ahead as if it's a game. Maybe it is?

'We should talk one day, Eden,' I say, and she curls her lip in disgust as if I've just suggested we take drugs and go out murdering squirrels. 'Seriously. I mean it. We should.'

'Why now?' Eden flings at me. 'Why now, after almost two years?'

I want to say that there is nobody else who knows why I wake up angry almost every day of my life, who remembers what I remember. I want to say that it's because I miss her, every bit as much as I miss Andie, Hasmita and Tasha. More, maybe.

OK, more, definitely.

I don't say any of this, though.

'Are you going to Lara's party?' I ask, as she walks away. 'Everybody says it will be cool. I'll see you there, maybe?'

'Don't hold your breath, Ryan Kelly,' she says.

## 18

## **Eden**

I have a paper-crane production line. By Wednesday morning there are more than fifty of them lined up along the living-room windowsill, all made from the bright patterned paper I bought in town.

I'd almost forgotten how restful folding cranes can be – the delicate, precise folding, the way you have to focus to get it right, to remember the sequence. I wonder if I would ever have the patience to fold a thousand of them, like in the school library book Andie found and read to us when we were ten. Our teacher had given the book to Andie when she first got into making paper cranes, because the story was all about a girl who made them.

I remember Andie dragging us off down the school playing fields one sunny lunchtime so she could share the story with us. It was the story of a Japanese girl called Sadako who got ill with leukaemia after the atom bomb was dropped on Hiroshima when she was a child. Japanese legend says that anyone who folds a thousand paper cranes will be granted a special wish. Sadako began to fold paper cranes, but she died before she reached her goal of a thousand, and her friends completed the task so that the cranes could be buried with her.

It was a very sad story . . . and a true one. I think it made us all cry, except possibly Ryan, though even he was wiping his eyes. He said it was just hay fever, but we didn't believe him.

I'd thought back then that a thousand paper cranes was an impossible number, but it probably isn't. I bet I could make that many and then some in all the time I spend not going to parties and not hanging out with friends.

The summer stretches ahead of me, vast and empty. Who am I kidding? I could probably make a million paper cranes. Would that grant me a special wish?

The doorbell rings, and I jump up, startled; it's a bit

late for the postman. I wander into the hall and open the front door a crack, and there on the landing outside the flat is Andie, her face lit up like it has its own source of sunshine.

'Hey!' she says, pushing the door open wide. 'I'm sorry I had to run yesterday . . . Something came up, but obviously, we have a lot of catching up to do. C'mon, Eden, don't look so surprised!'

I want to be gruff and cool, but I have never managed to be frosty with Andie, not for long – not even yesterday when I was numb with shock. I want to argue, to tell Andie she can't just turn up again after almost two years and expect me to drop everything for her, but there is no argument at all. Of course I'll drop everything for her. I always did; I always will.

'You going to invite me in, then?' she teases.

'No point,' I say. 'When did you ever wait for an invitation? You're going to come in anyway. You always do. At least, you used to!'

Andie is inside now, scoping out the hall. 'Your mum decorated,' she observes. 'Nice. How is she? Still working at the medical centre?'

'No . . . no, she's based at the drop-in centre in town, now,' I say. 'It's a better job – more money, but she works long hours. But yeah . . . we decorated the flat. Got rid of the red wine stain, y'know?'

'Do you hear much from your dad?' she asks, and I laugh and shake my head.

'A card on my birthday; cash at Christmas,' I tell her. 'I went down to London for a week last summer holidays, but it was all kind of awkward . . .'

Andie looks sad. 'I'm sorry,' she says. 'Sorry I haven't been here for you. I wish we'd kept in touch, Eden, really I do. Shall we go through to your room?'

It's like the last two years have never happened . . . me and Andie, holed up in my room, drinking orange juice with ice and talking about everything under the sun. She tries out my eyeliner, picks up a red scarf from my dressing table and ties it in her hair. There are no awkward silences – Andie wants to know everything.

'How's Ryan? What's he like these days?' she demands. 'Don't tell me . . . I bet he's got all the girls falling for him.'

'Not so much,' I say. 'He's turned bad boy, kind of. He's always in trouble.'

Andie frowns. 'Seriously? I can't imagine that. What happened?'

The Heart Club turned into the Broken Heart Club, that's what happened. We fell apart when Andie went away, and nothing has ever been the same again.

I don't say this, of course.

'I blame hormones,' I quip. 'Boys have them too, y'know . . .'

'Suppose,' Andie says with a grin. 'Hey, remember when we fell out over Ryan? What on earth was *that* all about?'

Nausea rises up inside me. What is Andie trying to do? She knows why we fell out over Ryan, knows how much trouble it caused. Surely she knows this is one topic we can't open up and talk about; it has the power to pull us apart all over again.

And of course I remember. I don't think I'll ever forget . . .

I close my eyes, trying to blot out the memories of Andie's eleventh birthday party, the night of the fall-out that broke us all apart. I try to push the memories away, but they're there in my head as fresh as if it were yesterday.

Andie, ice cold with fury, handing me her mobile to call home, my voice shaking as I told Mum I'd hurt my ankle and didn't want to stay at the sleepover. Tasha and Hasmita wiping the tears from Andie's eyes, torn between comforting the birthday girl and defending me. Ryan shaking his head and telling Andie she was out of order, that he thought better of her than this.

'It didn't mean anything, Andie,' I'd sobbed. 'I'd never, ever do anything to hurt you, you know that! You're my best friend!'

'You used to be,' she'd spat back at me. 'You've destroyed all that, now. I hate you, Eden, I *hate* you! I never want to see you again!'

My eyes snap open, my heart racing. The past slides away and I'm back in my bedroom again, Andie sitting cross-legged on the end of my bed the way she has so many times before.

'Hey, dreamer!' she says, nudging me gently. 'Aren't you listening? I was talking about that time we fell out over Ryan.'

I force a laugh. 'That? Old news, Andie,' I say. 'Water under the bridge. Ryan really isn't the person we thought he was. Bit of a loser. I never see him any more, and I can't say I miss him.'

Andie looks surprised at that.

'That's a shame,' she says. 'We were all so close, once –
but stuff changes, I know. Oh well! No boyfriends now,
then? No secret crushes?'

I shake my head, pushing back the bad memories.

'No . . . I've sworn off boys,' I tell her. 'I am so not
interested . . .'

Andie's eyes widen, and I can feel my cheeks begin to
burn. She has always been able to see right through me,
suss how I feel even when I don't know myself. How can
that be, after all this time? And how can a chance encounter with Ryan have me dreaming of a time when I thought
he was the coolest, cutest boy in the world? I was so, so hurt
that first day at Moreton Park, when he blanked me in the
corridor. How can I push that hurt aside just because he
has bothered to speak to me for once in two years? Am I
that weak, that pathetic? It's bizarre.

'Hey – there is someone, isn't there?' Andie says, softly.
'I can tell . . . you're blushing! Oh, Eden! Who is it? Anyone
I know?'

I hope she can't sense my panic and I really, really hope
she can't read my mind.

'No! There's nobody, Andie. Or just movie stars and characters in books, anyhow! Do they count? I'm way too busy for real-life boys. I have school work, and . . . stuff. Y'know. Friends.'

'OK, OK, stop digging, I believe you,' Andie says. 'I was going to ask about friends; how's Hasmita getting on at that fancy new school? And Tasha – is she fluent in French yet? Has she settled?'

My throat aches suddenly, as if I'm trying to swallow a slice of glass.

'Eden?'

'I don't see Hasmita much, these days,' I admit. 'Actually, I don't really see her at all. And Tasha . . . I emailed her a few times, at the beginning, but she never replied. We've sort of lost touch. How about you?'

Andie's face is sad now, her blue eyes shadowed. 'I haven't kept in touch either,' she says sadly. 'I wish I had. So . . . the Heart Club fell apart. That sucks. Who d'you hang out with now?'

I think about naming Chloe, Flick and Ima, but I have never lied to Andie and I am not about to start now.

'I don't, much,' I tell her. 'Friendship is overrated.'

Andie's eyes flash with anger, and then her arms are round me, hauling me in for a long, warm hug that smells of vanilla. That shard of glass is stuck in my throat again.

'What are we going to do with you, Eden?' she says at last, holding me at arm's length. 'Looks like I came back just in time!'

'Oh, I've missed you, Andie,' I whisper. 'So much!'

'Well, obviously!' she says. 'Who wouldn't? But I hate that you don't see the others any more and I hate that you've gone all loner on me. Not good, Eden, not good. Time we changed all that. Deal?'

'It's not that easy . . .'

'Easy?' Andie echoes. 'Who said it would be easy? Who cares? You need friends, Eden, and if I'm not around you'll have to find some others . . . Hey! What's this?'

She picks up the invitation to Lara's party, thrown down on my dressing table among a muddle of notebooks, pens and pencils. I grab it, but it's too late, Andie's eyes are sparkling.

'A party!' she declares. 'Lara's party? She's cool . . . and she has a cute elder brother, too, if I remember. Are you going? Eden, you have to!'

I try to argue. I explain that I can't go, that I don't do parties, have nobody to go with. I tell her I have nothing to wear, wouldn't know what to say, but Andie isn't in the mood for excuses. She jumps to her feet, rifles through my wardrobe, pulling a face at the black tops and jeans, the shapeless hoodies.

'I see what you mean,' she says, mock-outraged. 'What's with all this monochrome? I'm not against the Goth look, Eden, you know I'm not, but all this black . . . it's just not you, is it? Not the you I used to know and love, anyhow. Doesn't it make you feel drab and dull? Doesn't it make you feel sad? Doesn't it drain the life right out of you?'

I chew my lip, unable to meet her eyes. 'It's how I feel, these days, that's all . . .'

Andie looks stern. 'Why is the most beautiful girl I know hiding away in baggy, shapeless monochrome stuff?' she demands, sorting the hoodies and baggy jeans into a towering pile. 'These clothes are crimes against fashion! Where's the colour, where's the style? I guess some of these are OK . . .'

She puts my red skinny jeans in a separate pile, then adds a couple of little T-shirts, a short black skating skirt, frayed summer shorts and some striped fingerless mittens.

'These have potential,' she says. 'A bit of personality. But really – seriously – the rest has to go, Eden. I'm not joking. Bin the lot!'

'I *like* my clothes,' I argue, although I'm not sure I actually do, not really. They are chosen for their ordinariness, their dullness, and right now that seems a little bit sad. 'At least I used to . . .'

Andie flops down beside me on the bed.

'Maybe it's time things changed around here,' she declares. 'We'll sort it out, all of it. We'll go shopping, get you something to wear . . . it'll be fun!'

I smile, in spite of myself.

'Will you come with me? Not just shopping, but to the party?'

Andie rolls her eyes.

'Oh, go on then,' she says.

## 19

# Ryan

The next time I go running, I head out past the school. It's not as satisfying to lope past the gates now that the place is shut up for summer, but I stifle a smile as I turn along the street to Miss Smith's place, Rocket at my side.

As I enter through the broken gate, I can see that last week's work is looking good. Rocket has a quick explore and then settles on the grass in a patch of sun. It's very long grass, almost knee high and full of weeds. Rocket looks like he is in a jungle, and I find myself wondering if I can borrow a strimmer to get it cut, because that would make the whole garden about a million times neater.

Then there's the pond, which is a project in itself. I notice Miss Smith standing at the window, her hand raised shakily against the glass, and I wave back, grinning.

I find an ancient watering can rusting in a corner and track down the outside tap. I give everything a good soaking, including my trainers, because the watering can has a hole. I tie an unruly rose bush back against the fence with a few remnants of string from my pocket, then go over to the bird feeder and fill it up with peanuts bought from the corner shop earlier. The gnarled little tree may be ancient and frazzled, but at least now when she looks out of the window the old lady will be able to watch birds flitting around, perching and feeding.

I'm just about to leave when the door creaks open again and Miss Smith appears carrying the same chipped blue mug as last week. 'Peter!' she calls. 'I've made you some hot chocolate!'

I am not sure how to explain that I am not Peter, or that I don't trust her hot chocolate, so I walk over and take it anyway. This time it turns out to be boiled water, which is an improvement on last week's old teabag. I take a pretend sip, smiling.

Rocket saunters across, tail wagging, soft brown eyes fixed on Miss Smith.

'I wouldn't leave you out, would I, Patch?' she says, unfurling a claw-like hand to offer Rocket a broken Rich Tea biscuit. 'Here you go. Good boy! Do you remember, Peter, when you first found Patch? A stray, he was, beaten and half-starved and full of fleas, but you were determined to give him a home. We put him in the tin bath and hosed him down with the watering can and washed him with lye soap until he was clean. I never knew a dog so loved! You'd give him the rind off your bacon, swipe the bones I'd bought for the stock pot before I got a chance to cook them and give them to Patch. And don't think I don't know he used to sneak on to the bed with you at night! I knew, all right. They were good days, weren't they, Peter?'

I have no clue at all what Miss Smith is talking about, but it seems rude to say so.

'They were the best days ever,' I agree.

Rocket eats the biscuit carefully, politely, and allows Miss Smith to pat his head. While she is distracted, I pour the boiled water into a flower bed.

'Do you have a lawnmower?' I ask.

'Of course I do,' Miss Smith says. 'You should know that, Peter. It's in the shed, where it always is.'

'Right. I'll swing by another day and cut the grass for you, OK?'

'Bring Patch, won't you?' she says.

I promise that I will.

## 20

### Eden

I cannot remember when I last had this much fun; Andie can make me giggle with just one glance, one raised eyebrow, one word. She is ruthlessly honest but a hundred per cent on my side, and that's the best kind of clothes shopping companion you could ever wish to have.

'Our mission is to get some colour into your life,' Andie declares. 'Some cute. Trust me on this; you will look awesome.'

'I don't like to stand out,' I argue.

'You were born to stand out,' Andie insists. 'I promise. Don't make me paint your face with yellow poster paint all over again.'

'OK, OK, but not a dress,' I plead. 'I am really not a dress kind of person these days. And I like dark colours . . .'

Andie ignores me and gathers up an armful of rainbow bright garments before steering me into the changing room. She comes in too, my own personal stylist, and the shop assistant doesn't even bat an eyelid.

'Try it with this belt,' she says, hauling in a scarlet prom dress with a fancy punched-leather cinch belt and a frown. 'No, maybe not. Try this silver mini . . . very slinky! No, no; it's not working, you look like you're wrapped in tinfoil . . . I'm not sure why. You have the figure for it, you're really tall and willowy; you could literally wear anything. Anything except that scarlet one. And the silver. OK, shall we try the body-con one?'

'Do we have to?'

'We have to.'

Struggling into the mini dress is a little bit like trying to put on a wetsuit, and the result is just as unflattering. I look like a six-year-old wearing her mum's underslip. Not good.

'It's not working,' Andie concurs. 'Weird. Maybe with heels?'

'Not a chance,' I say.

'Actually, I think it's the hair.' She frowns. 'I mean, it's interesting, but the colour drains your skin tone, looks all wrong. It just doesn't look like *you*. Should we do something with it?'

I peer into the changing room mirror. 'I need to touch up my roots,' I say. 'That might help. We'll go to Superdrug next. But the dresses aren't working because I just don't do cutesy or glam; how about you let *me* choose?'

Andie pulls a face, but she trails back into the shop with me. 'No black,' she instructs. 'You're not in mourning, are you? And no more shapeless hoodies – this is a party. You need to get out of your comfort zone!'

In the end, I pick out a blue and white striped Breton top and a pair of faded denim shorts with bib and braces attached. Andie complains loudly about how dungarees are not a party item as we haul them back to the changing rooms, but everything together actually looks good; it's not what I'd usually wear, but I like it, and Andie seems to approve.

'Not bad,' she admits. 'You need coloured tights, obviously, but the striped top is cool and the shorts show off your legs . . . yep, it's a good look. Tomboyish but cute. Very you! And I bet your crush will love it.'

'Stop it, Andie!' I cut in. 'I don't have a crush; I told you!'

Andie just raises an eyebrow, her mouth twitching into a smirk.

'Will Ryan be there?' she asks. 'It'll be weird seeing him after all this time . . .'

'I don't think Ryan does parties,' I say, shutting down this line of conversation even though I have no clue at all whether Ryan is a party animal or not. I just don't want anything to derail my renewed bond with Andie, and getting tangled up with Ryan seems like the fastest way to do it.

'Hey – how come I'm the only one being dressed up and thrown to the lions here? Are you buying something new for the party?'

'I don't think so; I've already got a couple of things that would do,' she says vaguely. 'We're here for you, Eden, and if I have anything to do with it, you're going to look amazing! Look, I'm going to grab some bits and pieces to finish the look . . .'

I check my wallet to make sure my birthday cash is going to be enough, but everything we've picked is in the summer sale and I reckon I'm good. Mum would have subbed me some extra money, I know, but I haven't mentioned Andie's reappearance to her. I know she wouldn't understand. When Andie went away I was in bits for ages; how would she react now that my best friend is back on the scene?

I like to think she'd be happy for me, but I doubt it somehow. She'd just think that Andie will upset me all over again, and I know that's not going to happen.

I'm queuing for the till with the top and dungarees when Andie appears with teal-blue tights, a polka-dot scarf to tie in my hair and a whole load of beaded bangles. I take a deep breath and buy the lot, and then we head for Superdrug for hair dye.

'Black Beauty,' Andie says disapprovingly, reading the packet in my hand. 'Seriously? Is this stuff aimed at people or horses? Are you sure this is your colour, Eden? Black can look really dramatic on some people, but I think it's kind of draining on you. If you want to dye your hair, how about something brighter, more fun? Ultra Violet, or

Magenta Madness, even Sizzling Satsuma; try something different. Go crazy!'

I hesitate, uncertain.

'Or you could just go back to your real hair colour,' Andie suggests gently, picking up a packet called Light Golden Brown. 'No more roots to worry about. And we already know it looks awesome. What d'you say?'

'But I sort of like it black!'

'I always tell you the truth, don't I?' Andie says. 'I always have and I always will. Black isn't all that flattering on you, that's all. It makes you look pale and washed out, kind of sad – you don't look like *you* any more!'

But I am not me any more, not really. Can't Andie see that?

'Come on,' she coaxes. 'Let me fix your hair, get it back to its natural colour. It'll look fantastic!'

'Are you sure?' I waver.

'I'm sure. I'll come over tomorrow and do it for you, and we'll go to the party together.'

Andie gets her way, just as she always did.

I don't mind – it feels so good to be with her again. We walk down the High Street arm in arm and I can feel myself beginning to thaw, like the Arctic tundra when spring comes around. My heart, numb and frozen for the longest time, is starting to melt. With Andie around, I'm changing, softening, coming alive once more.

21

# Ryan

I'm in the park with Buzz, Chris and a bunch of lads from school, supposedly for a five-a-side footy match, but I made the mistake of bringing Rocket along, so things are not going smoothly. Rocket keeps sprinting on to the pitch and stealing the ball, which is not making me – or him – popular.

'Get that stupid dog out of here!' a lad called Sullie yells. 'Ryan, get a grip! He's wrecking the game!'

'He's just playing,' I argue. 'Don't take it so seriously!'

'Football *is* serious,' Sullie growls. 'D'you have to play the clown the whole time, Ryan? C'mon, this isn't funny!'

'It is from where I'm standing,' I say, as Rocket shoots

through Sullie's legs and launches himself at a boy called Mitch, unbalancing him and knocking him to the ground. 'He's our best striker; our secret weapon!'

Sullie folds his arms, a few of the others behind him. Mitch, still sprawled on the grass, is being licked to death by Rocket.

'I'm red-carding you, Ryan,' Sullie says. 'Next time, don't bring the dog.'

Honestly, some people have no sense of humour.

'See you after the match,' Buzz calls. 'Hang around, mate – once we've thrashed these losers, we can go have some fun. Meet you in the cafe – you can get the Cokes in!'

I just laugh and haul Rocket away, heading for the cafe. 'You're a liability, mutt,' I tell him. 'A menace. Bit like me . . .'

I'm almost at the park cafe when I see Eden Banks walking across the grass. She looks different – she's striding along, swinging a couple of New Look carrier bags, her steps light. Her head is thrown back, as if she's looking at the blue summer sky, lost in some kind of a happy dream. I remember how beautiful she looks when she's smiling, how her face lights up from inside.

I haven't seen her look like this since – well, not since the Heart Club broke into pieces. The sight is so bizarre that I falter and stall and come to a complete standstill.

It's almost like seeing the old Eden again.

Rocket looks up at me like he can't work me out at all, and then his eyes follow mine and he catches sight of Eden. His ears prick up and cogs are clearly turning in his doggy brain, because the next minute he pulls away from me and he's off, the lead trailing behind him.

'Rocket!' I yell. 'Rocket, come back!'

He ignores me, ploughing right through the middle of a carefully planted flower bed of big yellow daisy-like flowers.

'Rocket! No!'

It's no good, though. There are moments when Rocket lives up to his name, and this is one of them. What is going through his mind? Ice cream, I realize. He is quite a smart dog, when you think about it.

I decide to change tack.

'Eden!' I yell. 'Eden, watch out!'

It's too late, of course.

I see her snap out of the dream, her face turning towards

me. Then she spots Rocket, rampaging across the grass, and before she has a chance he launches himself at her, toppling her over on to the ground.

I cringe. The Eden I know these days will not be impressed with such an unbridled display of affection.

I break into a sprint, closing the distance between us, but by the time I reach them, Eden is laughing and stroking Rocket. His tail is swishing back and forth like crazy, like a windscreen wiper on overdrive.

I launch into a whole bunch of apologies.

'Sorry – he doesn't mean it; he's overenthusiastic. Badly trained, I suppose. That's my fault. We got thrown out of dog-training classes, me for smoking round the back of the church hall, Rocket for stealing a whole trayful of dog treats . . .'

'You're a walking disaster zone, aren't you?' she says, looking up at me. 'What were you smoking for?'

I shrug. 'It was a phase I was going through. A short phase. I suppose the bad rep made it more appealing, but I stopped in the end because it was too expensive. Also, it made my fingers go yellow and my breath got stinky. Bad times.'

'I'll say,' Eden agrees, getting to her feet and gathering up her carrier bags.

'Well, sorry again,' I say. 'Rocket gets carried away.'

'It's never the dogs, always the owners,' she comments, which seems a little harsh. 'He's a nice dog, actually. Friendly.'

'So am I,' I point out. 'Although not a dog, obviously. I'm human. Slightly accident-prone, attracted to trouble, but basically well-meaning and almost always friendly.'

Eden sighs, unimpressed.

'Tell that to the little old lady you threw a javelin at,' she says with a sniff.

'That story was wildly exaggerated,' I argue. 'In my defence, the javelin went into the pond. The pond had no fish; nobody was scared or harmed. And the little old lady and me are best mates now, as a matter of fact. I've been tidying up her garden for her. I don't suppose you have access to a strimmer, do you? Or a hedge trimmer?'

'You're weird,' she says.

'You and me both,' I retaliate. 'Embrace it, Eden. Weird is the new cool.'

She pats Rocket again, throws me a disdainful glance

and walks away, shoulders back, carrier bags swinging. There is a definite spring in her step; I can see it.

'Hey – are you going to Lara's party tomorrow?' I shout after her. 'Hope so! See you there, Eden!'

'Not if I see you first,' she yells over her shoulder, and I have a feeling she means it.

## 22

## Eden

It's Friday, and Mum reminds me she won't be home till late; she's going out with Jo and the girls after work.

'I'm going out, too,' I say. 'A party at Lara's house. You remember Lara, from primary?'

Mum's eyes open wide, as if I've just told her I will be headlining at Glastonbury.

'A party?' she echoes. 'You're going to a party?'

'Yep, that's right. You were saying earlier in the week that I should get out more, mix with people a bit. I just decided you were right, that's all!'

Mum is floundering, 'But . . . oh, Eden, that's brilliant, really, but when will you be back? Who will you be with?

Do you need a lift home? I wish you'd mentioned it earlier!'

'It was kind of a last-minute decision,' I say. 'I knew you were going out, so I decided I'd get brave and go. I thought you'd be pleased!'

'I am pleased! What are you going to wear? Shall I meet you afterwards, bring you home?'

'It's all sorted, Mum,' I tell her. 'I bought a few bits yesterday in town with my birthday money, and I'm going with a friend. I think we're getting a lift back, but if not, I'll text you, OK?'

'Which friend?'

Mum's face is shining with relief and happiness, and I know that a mention of Andie would wipe that smile clean away. A little white lie won't hurt, will it?

'I'm going with Chloe and Flick and Ima,' I say. 'They're lovely – you'd like them.'

'Oh! OK! Well, then, have a great time, sweetheart,' she says. 'I'm so pleased you're going, really I am – I'm proud of you, Eden. You'll have fun, you wait and see!'

I'm not having fun a few hours later, though. My hair is coated with sticky dye and wrapped in tinfoil to avoid drips. While I'm helpless, Andie is painting my nails a rich turquoise shade, complete with glitter sprinkles.

I feel like Cinderella being transformed for the ball. The way Andie is going, nobody will even recognize me, but that idea is strangely exhilarating. I imagine myself running away on the last stroke of midnight, leaving one solitary Converse trainer on the garden path. 'Who was that girl?' they will ask themselves. 'Where did she come from?'

An alarm starts to buzz on my phone and Andie drags me back to the sink to wash away the hair dye. When she's finished, she shows me how to blow-dry my hair upside down, scrunching to make the most of the waves. My hair feels strange, but she drapes a towel over the mirror so I can't check on progress, then takes the straighteners from my dressing table and drops them in the bin. I fish them out again, exasperated, and hide them in a drawer.

'Your hair is perfect just the way it is – or was, before your dodgy Goth phase,' Andie scolds. 'And now we've staged a rescue, you have to resist the temptation to dye it black and straighten it. Seriously, I'm all for experiments, and Goth can look awesome, but I'm telling you the truth here. It didn't suit you, Eden. You looked like Morticia from the Addams Family!'

'Thanks a bunch!' I say.

'I'm trying to help,' she says, brandishing the kitchen scissors as she peers critically at my fringe. 'Be grateful! OK, it's a close call, but I think maybe we should let that ratty fringe grow out.'

'I like my fringe!' I argue. 'And it's not ratty!'

'You hide behind it,' she counters. 'And trust me, Eden, your hiding days are over.'

I stick my tongue out at Andie, laughing.

'Don't ever be a hairdresser,' I warn her. 'You're way too bossy!'

'Don't worry, I won't,' she replies, and her eyes look shadowed, just for a moment. Then she's back on form, turning up the music – old stuff, happy stuff from the days when we used to hang out and not the crashy, clashy misery-rock I usually listen to.

'So . . . I was thinking hair slides, but actually, if I tie this scarf in your hair it's kind of vintage-cool and tomboyish at the same time, and it hides the fringe. OK, time to get changed and then I can do your make-up.'

'But I want to see my hair!'

'Not yet. It's gorgeous, just trust me on that!'

I give in. I turn my back on Andie, change into my new stuff and give a little twirl. She nods her approval, sitting me down beside the dressing table to get started on the make-up. I lean back and relax into it. We spent hours doing exactly this when we were eight or nine, stealing our mothers' make-up and taking it in turns to play at being guinea pig for each other's makeover skills. We channelled everything from Lady Gaga glam to zombie apocalypse, with a side order of vampire chic. Andie is taking this just as seriously.

'You don't need foundation,' she tells me as the make-up brush strokes shadow on my eyelids. 'No spots or anything, just those freckles, which are super-cute. And that heavy black eyeliner is OK, but I'm going to use brown and keep it natural, OK? Dark brown mascara, too. And I'm using quite a vivid blue on your eyelids, and just a tiny smear of glitter, so we won't bother with lipstick because the eyes are the focus with this look. Hold still!'

I try not to think too much, or worry too much. Andie knows what she's doing. The idea of the looming party terrifies me, but my best friend has my back, just like she always did. It might actually be fun.

A few minutes later, I am standing in front of the mirror, ready for the big reveal. I've slipped Ryan's tattered paper crane into the pocket of my shorts for good luck, and when Andie whips the towel away from the glass I see my reflection at last, a slim, grinning girl with golden-brown wavy hair and a cute, quirky outfit. The teal-blue tights make my legs look longer and the eye make-up has opened up my eyes – made them look wide, sparkly, startlingly blue. Amazingly, I like it. I look like me, but a better, brighter version of the me I haven't seen in years.

Maybe I will chuck out the hair dye and straighteners after all.

For a moment, my eyes blur and then I square my shoulders and blink back the tears, because I don't cry, can't cry, daren't cry.

'Like it?' Andie asks, anxious.

'Love it!'

I throw my arms round her and hold on tight, as if I might never let go.

23

# Ryan

I forget about Lara's party until I'm crossing the park with Buzz and Chris on Friday evening and see Chloe, Flick and Ima all dolled up in bright dresses and fancy shoes.

'Hello, girls!' Buzz leers. 'Going somewhere nice? Can we come?'

'In your dreams,' Chloe snaps.

'Playing hard to get?' Chris growls. 'C'mon, lighten up! Tell us where you're going – we'll come too. Spice things up a bit!'

'Yeah, right,' Ima says under her breath, tugging at her sparkly headscarf so it hides a little more of her face. I don't blame her, to be honest. Buzz and Chris are a kind of clunky when it comes to chat-up lines.

'Ignore my friends,' I say with a sigh, stepping forward. 'What they mean to say is, hello, how are you? Nice evening, isn't it?'

At that moment, Rocket appears from out of the bushes, skidding to a halt in front of them, panting wolfishly. This spoils things slightly, and all three girls take a step back, awkward, wary. Their eyes skim from Rocket to me, and they do not look impressed, In fact, if I didn't know better, I'd say they were scared, but that's crazy. Buzz and Chris are boneheads, sure, but I'm just the sidekick, the comic relief. In spite of the javelin rumours, I'm not actually scary, surely?

'So,' I say, smiling broadly to put them at ease. 'Going to the party?'

'Er, no,' Chloe responds. 'Maybe. Whatever . . .'

'What party?' Buzz grumbles, slightly put out. 'I didn't get an invite!'

'Lara Keehoe's party,' Chris says. 'Who needs an invite? We'll gatecrash – might be fun!'

Buzz runs a hand through his hair and fixes on his

scariest grin. 'Cool,' he says. 'Let's go, ladies! The night is young!'

The girls look genuinely terrified at the thought, and scaring girls is really not my style. I jump to the rescue.

'Nah, it's still early,' I tell my friends. 'The party won't warm up for hours. Besides, I'm not taking Rocket to a rave. I'm gonna go home, have a shower, get changed; who knows, it could be my lucky night!'

'Yeah, yeah, we should spruce up first,' Chris agrees. 'Obviously. Look our best for the chicks.'

'I'll nick some cans from my dad,' Buzz decides. 'Or a bottle of cider, maybe. Get things going a bit!'

Chloe, Flick and Ima are edging away, trying to escape. I fall into step beside them, throw a wink at Buzz and Chris to try to keep them at a distance.

'Let me and Rocket escort you through the park,' I say, switching on the charm. 'You get some very dodgy characters lurking around at this time of the evening.'

'Like you and your mates,' Ima says.

'Me?' I protest, mock-outraged. 'I am a hundred per cent kind and courteous to others. Most of the time, anyway. Unless they happen to be teachers . . .'

'Just go away,' Chloe says, a note of pleading in her voice. 'We're fine, seriously. We don't need any help from you and your halfwit sidekicks!'

'Chloe!' I argue, pretending to be devastated. 'My friends may be a little slow to take a hint, but they're harmless really. Most of the time. And me – well, let's just say I'm misunderstood. I wanted to ask – you *are* going to the party? Everyone's going, yeah? It's meant to be the party of the year . . .'

'So I've heard,' Flick says, noncommittal.

I lower my voice. 'So. Do you happen to know . . . will Eden Banks be there?'

The girls raise their eyebrows, exchange amused looks. With one sentence, I have morphed from scary schoolboy delinquent to lovesick loser. They are much more comfortable with that.

'She said she might go,' Ima admits. 'We asked her last week at school and she said no, but then we saw her earlier in the week and she said she'd see us there. Definitely.'

'Although knowing Eden, she probably won't,' Chloe adds. 'She's a bit of a loner, isn't she? We try to be friendly, but she pushes us away.'

'I know the feeling.'

The girls watch me carefully, in case further gossip might be available. I feel like an exhibit in the zoo.

'Does your dog bite?' Ima asks. 'I heard it was a pit bull cross . . .'

I take hold of Rocket's collar, but his tail is wagging so hard it's a miracle he doesn't explode with joy. He's just a mongrel, something daft crossed with something hairy; there's nothing growly or dangerous in his breeding. Still, it's too good a rumour to ignore.

'Pit bull crossed with wolf,' I say casually, and Ima's mouth drops open.

'Is it true you attacked an old lady with a school javelin?' Flick demands.

'It was only a small graze,' I quip. 'She was getting on my nerves . . .'

'That's disgusting,' Flick whispers, outraged. 'Why haven't you been expelled? Why wasn't it in the papers?'

'The head's scared of me.' I shrug. 'He hushed it up, and obviously the old lady's in no state to go telling anyone. Besides, the head's seen my criminal record; he knows he could be next on the hit list!'

I almost feel guilty then as the girls grab each other, faces blank with horror, and hurry away along the path. Almost. The thing about having a bad rep at school is that what people don't actually know, they invent, and I choose to laugh at the rumours rather than let them upset me.

As I watch, Ima looks back over her shoulder, eyes narrowed. I can see disbelief in her eyes, the trace of a smile on her lips. She suspects I'm winding them up, but she is not totally sure.

'See you at the party, girls!' I yell, and they screech and break into a run.

## 24

# Eden

'How long is it since we went to a party together?' Andie asks as we walk arm in arm towards Lara's house in the golden evening light. 'Does my birthday camp-out count? Probably not, because it was just us five. It must have been Tasha's leaving party, then.'

Tasha's party . . . how could I forget it? It'd been just days before Andie's birthday, and everyone had been there. Although it was a bittersweet occasion because we were sad about Tasha moving to France, it was still a pretty cool party.

'Awww,' I say. 'That was so much fun. So happy and so sad, all at the same time. Remember the cake we made that looked like the French flag? And how the grown-ups got tipsy, and your mum and dad danced into the washing line and got all tangled up?'

'Great party,' Andie says wistfully. 'Poor Mum and Dad . . . that was so funny! I really miss those times. It seems so long ago, now. I wish you were still in touch with Tasha. I always thought you guys would stay close forever . . .'

'It's hard to stay close when there's a sea between you,' I point out. 'I tried, Andie. I emailed loads of times. She never answered, not once.'

'That's so sad,' she sighs. 'How about a letter? One last try, for me?'

I sigh. 'I'll try,' I promise. 'I loved those days, too, Andie. We had so much fun, didn't we?'

'We did,' Andie says. 'I can't believe it all fell apart. I can't believe Ryan turned bad boy, or that Tash went silent. I can't believe Hasmita just dropped you . . .'

'Well, it's true,' I tell her. 'The Heart Club turned into the Broken Heart Club. My best friends ditched me, pure and simple.'

Andie's eyes mist with tears.

'It's so sad, Eden,' she says. 'I really hoped you'd all still be friends. Friends forever, that's what we said, right? Promise me, Eden, that you'll try to make some new friends at this party. For me?'

I frown. 'But . . . I thought we were going together?'

'We are, but that doesn't mean we have to stick to each other like glue, does it? The whole point is to get you socializing again, and while you're doing that, maybe I'll catch up with a few old friends – see what's been happening while I've been gone!'

This is not quite what I had in mind, but Andie is determined.

'Promise you'll try,' she says, and I find myself promising.

We've reached the top of Lara's street, silence falling around us like a cloak. Andie reaches for my hand and squeezes it hard, which somehow makes my heart ache. The party doesn't seem important now, though already I can tell which house it is because of the steady thud of music carrying on the evening air.

There's a bus stop up ahead, and we duck inside, sit down side by side.

Andie was always so much more than just a friend to me – she was my soul sister. Without her, a part of me shrivelled up and died. I can feel that part of me coming back to life, and that scares me a little.

What if I have to go through all that hurt again?

'It's still early,' Andie says. 'We can talk, if you want. About Ryan, about Tash and Hasmita; about us. There's still so much I want to say, need to say, and there isn't much time left.'

Not much time left? What does that even mean? Nausea rolls through me suddenly, and the world seems to tilt a little on its axis.

'It's difficult,' Andie is saying. 'I had to go away. I had no choice. You know that, don't you? Eden?'

My eyes feel gritty, sore. It's probably some kind of allergy to the glittery eyeshadow, but my throat is aching too, like I've been swallowing razor blades.

'I know,' I choke out. 'It's just . . . I miss you so much, Andie. It's been two years; I'd given up hope of ever hearing from you again.'

'I just haven't been able to get in touch,' she says quietly. 'It was hard; I can't really explain. Friends forever, and all that.'

But I don't believe in that any more. It's a fairy story, and a cruel one.

'Are you back to stay?' I ask in a whisper. 'Can things go back to the way they were?'

'That's not possible,' she answers. 'I wish it was! I've told you already, I'm only here for a few days . . . I'm sorry!'

'When do you go?'

Andie smiles and shakes her head. 'Soon. I don't really know . . .'

'You don't know? What kind of an answer is that?' I'm angry now, needy. Seeing Andie has shown me just what I've been missing. If she goes away again, I don't know how I will cope.

*Not much time left . . .*

'It's not up to me,' Andie is saying. 'I have to go back. I'm sorry, Eden – you know that!'

'Will you stay in touch, though?' I ask, hating the pleading tone in my voice. 'Texts? Messages? Phone calls, maybe?'

Andie's blue eyes mist with tears. 'Maybe,' she says. 'I don't want to make it any harder for you; maybe a clean break is best.'

'No!' I beg. 'Please, Andie?'

'I'll try. I will. I'm so sorry, Eden.'

A bus draws up and a crowd of teenagers spill out on to

the pavement. I know most of them vaguely from school, but they don't recognize me at all, or Andie either. My new look must be pretty dramatic. From sad-faced Goth girl to quirky teen tomboy in less than twenty-four hours . . . which one is the real me?

I have no idea.

It's pretty clear that the gang of kids are heading for Lara's party – they are drawn towards the music and the lights like moths to a flame. We watch them laughing and clowning about as they head up the street, as if they haven't a care in the world. They probably haven't.

I'm filled with a terrible sadness. I am going to lose Andie all over again.

'Hey,' she says, nudging me with an elbow. 'We have a party to get to, right?'

I couldn't care less about the party right now, but I fix a smile on my face and I'm rewarded with an answering grin on Andie's.

'C'mon, trouble,' Andie quips. 'Let's go!'

We link arms and walk along the street towards Lara's house.

25

# Ryan

Back in the old days, Andie used to bribe me to come to sleepovers with promises of apple pie and pizza and permission to retreat to a quiet corner and read Harry Potter if I got fed up with clowning around and playing the idiot. I never did get fed up, though; not really. When the Heart Club were together, boredom was never an option.

I had the best of all worlds . . . the freedom to play footy, to skateboard and play Xbox games about zombies and car chases, and then to step into a whole different world with Andie, Eden, Tasha and Hasmita.

I liked that world a lot, obviously. The Heart Club girls were different from my boy mates; gentler, wilder, kinder. It was like having four crazy sisters who knew you better than anyone else alive – or perhaps three crazy sisters and Eden. I liked her way too much, even then, and not in a sisterly kind of way.

By Year Six, I'd got to that awkward stage where I couldn't leave the house without spending ten minutes in front of the mirror with the comb and the hair gel. I'd been getting through cans of Lynx body spray at an alarming rate, and yet girls were not chasing me along the street or fainting at my feet. They sometimes pinched their noses and rolled their eyes if I came too close, and Tasha told me I was probably overdoing it with the Lynx, so I toned it down.

I was eleven years and three months old when I kissed Eden's ear at the camp-out sleepover. It had taken me that long to screw up the courage to make a move, and I thought she looked amazing that night – the most beautiful girl in the world.

I'd been aiming for her lips, but she saw me coming and I could see the panic in her eyes. She turned her face and

I ended up clumsily kissing her ear, but I didn't care at all because I heard her draw in a breath and felt her cheek burn warm against mine, her fingers curl round mine in the darkness.

'Ryan . . .' she whispered. 'I thought . . .'

I never did get to hear what she thought, sadly.

It all went wrong.

Andie saw us and went nuts, and all three of us fell out big time, with Tasha and Hasmita looking on helplessly, trying their best to make peace. Nightmare.

So yeah . . . parties.

I find my best pair of jeans, iron my vintage Nirvana T-shirt, slip on new Vans trainers. I shove some gel in my hair and drag a comb through it, stare at the mirror and wish I looked more . . . well, more something, anyway. I brush my teeth for five whole minutes, then gargle with mouthwash and go looking for chewing gum.

Parties are not my favourite way to spend a Friday night, but Buzz and Chris are set on a night of revelry and I may as well go along for the laugh. Besides, if Eden is there I might find a way to chip away the ice-maiden mask, see if I can find a way back to the girl I used to know.

I'm not sure if Lara's party is the right place to do this, but I am willing to try.

26

## Eden

Lara's front door stands wide open. A group of Year Ten boys are having some kind of break-dance competition on the front lawn. Inside the house, shrieks and whoops can be heard above the sound of the music, and the hallway looks so rammed with people I am not sure how we will ever get in.

I would turn round and walk away right now if Andie weren't here with me, but she is here, so I square my shoulders and follow her along the path. One of the break-dance boys dips down to pick some kind of daisy flower from a flower bed and hands it to me as I pass.

'There, y'see? Proof that your new look is totally awesome and irresistible,' Andie quips. 'I didn't get one!'

'He was probably too in awe of you,' I say. 'You have that effect on boys. Oh, Andie, is this a good idea? There are way too many people here!'

'It's a very good idea,' she says. 'Trust me. C'mon!'

She takes my hand and leads me inside, elbowing her way through the crowd, people shoving and pushing past us.

'I smell pizza!' Andie yells gleefully. 'Just like old times! D'you think they'll have cheese and pineapple? Let's head for the kitchen!'

'What if we get separated?'

Andie just laughs. 'That's what parties are all about,' she tells me. 'We're here to talk to people, make new mates, have fun. Go with the flow, Eden! Don't worry about me, I'll be fine. I'll see you at the end of the night, and we can talk about it all, just like old times!'

Andie's hand slips away from mine and I find myself carried along in the crush of people like driftwood on the tide. I wash up in the kitchen, which is thankfully less crowded and a little quieter than the hallway. Chloe, Flick and Ima are helping Lara to set out food and mix up a lurid-looking fruit punch that seems to involve chopped apples, halved strawberries and bottles of lemonade, cherryade and cream soda.

Chloe, Flick and Ima seem not to notice me, but Lara, looking very grown up in a sparkly purple dress and high heels she can't quite balance on, looks up and does a double take. Her eyes widen and her mouth forms a perfect 'o'.

'Eden?' she says. 'Wow – is it you? You look so different! Like you used to, only more grown-up, obviously! I like it!'

The other three are staring now, as if they're seeing me for the first time. Maybe they are? I look back over my shoulder and spot Andie, still stuck in the hallway crush. She grins and waves her hand in the air as if telling me to relax, not to worry; knowing her, she'll have found a gaggle of old friends to chat to. Or new friends, maybe.

'Eden!' Chloe is saying. 'You made it! You actually came! I didn't think you would, and now here you are and I almost didn't recognize you – you look so different! Amazing!'

'Have you dyed your hair?' Flick wants to know. 'OMG! That colour really suits you! So cool!'

I try to say that it's my natural colour, but my words are lost as a burst of heavy bass and drums erupts in a nearby room.

'So glad you came!' Ima shouts into my ear. 'Here, have some fruit punch! Lara's brother's band are just kicking off in the living room.'

I take a paper cup of fruit punch from the kitchen table, still clutching the flower. I look back again at Andie, but she's in the middle of a big group, laughing, talking. I couldn't reach her if I tried. Maybe she's right – maybe I should try to make a few new friends?

'The band are awesome,' Lara tells me. 'And I'm not just saying that, they really, really are. C'mon, guys!'

She ducks back out into the hall, into the living room, Chloe and Flick in her wake. Ima waits, smiling, wanting to include me.

'Shall we go through?' she asks.

'OK, sure,' I say. 'I came with a friend, but I guess she'll work out where I am. Let's go see what they're like!'

I take a deep breath and step into the living room, into the magic.

27

# Ryan

The one advantage of having a reputation as a trouble-maker is that people step out of your way pretty fast. The crowd in the hallway parts to let Buzz, Chris and me pass through, and I feel like Moses parting the Red Sea.

My mates lead the way to the kitchen, shovel pizza into their mouths, taste the fruit punch and spit it out again in disgust at the lack of alcohol. Buzz starts ransacking the cupboards in search of something more interesting to add, and comes up with chilli sauce, cooking sherry and a jar of Branston Pickle.

'Have you even been invited?' one girl asks as he empties

them all into the punch while Chris stirs the foul brew. 'You think you're so tough, don't you? Idiots!'

'You love me really,' Buzz is saying as I abandon the kitchen and follow the sound of the music. The living room is a wonderland of fairy lights and strobes. Lara's brother and his band are squashed into the far corner, and they're hammering out a bright, happy R&B sound that has the whole room jumping. The floor is crammed with kids dancing and there's no way of getting to the front, so I climb on an armchair and perch on the back to get a better view.

I almost miss Eden at first. I'm scanning the room for a slouching Goth girl in black baggy clothes, but I get distracted by the cute girl in the dungaree shorts who is dancing with Chloe, Flick and Ima, her wavy golden brown hair flying out around her like a halo. I watch her move to the music, arms floating out around her, face lit up in different colours by the flickering strobes and fairy lights. I think she must be a friend of Chloe, Flick and Ima; someone from another school. I wonder who she reminds me of, and then my heart flips over and I jump down from the armchair and push through the crowd until I'm right in front of her.

'Eden!' I yell above the music. 'Eden! It's you!'

Her blue eyes light up for a moment, then the light shuts down again. She's standing still now, a slightly wilted flower dangling from one hand.

'Who else would I be?' she yells back.

'Funny,' I shout into her ear. 'You know exactly what I mean. You look amazing! I mean – well, you look like *you*!'

Chloe, Flick and Ima have stopped dancing, flanking Eden like bodyguards, shooting me death-stares. 'Is he bothering you?' Chloe asks Eden.

'Yes – no, I'm fine,' she yells back. 'Look, Ryan, I'm dancing and you're sort of in the way . . . .'

I grin. 'No I'm not – I'm dancing too!'

It's hard to strut your stuff when the room is packed to bursting, but I play it for laughs and exaggerate every movement, spinning and skanking and grooving like I'm in some kind of 1970s dance-off. At first, Eden and the girls look exasperated, annoyed, but I win them over and before long they're dancing round me and we're all laughing together. I think that dancing is probably as good as running for chasing away the anger, or maybe it's just that the band are so relentlessly happy, or because I'm making people laugh instead of scaring them.

Finally, the band announce their last song and I impro-
vise a jive routine, dancing with each of the girls in turn,
spinning and whirling them through the crowd. As the last
chords die away, I'm still holding Eden's hand, and somehow I don't want to let go.

'You're still an idiot underneath the tough guy act, Ryan
Kelly,' she says into my ear. 'Funny, though!'

'Thank you . . . I think!' I say, making a mock bow. 'I'm
wrecked. Shall we get a drink and cool down?'

Eden shrugs and looks over her shoulder anxiously, but
she allows me to tow her to the kitchen. Buzz and Chris
are thankfully nowhere to be seen. I bypass the spiked fruit
punch and pour two mugs of cherryade from a bottle on
the kitchen counter, but as more kids come in searching for
drinks, the mood darkens. Some are gagging at the revolt-
ing punch; some have sussed the taste of alcohol beyond
the chilli sauce and are knocking it back with abandon.
Things are going to get messy.

'This is crazy,' Eden says. 'I have to go, Ryan. Find the
friend I came with . . .'

But before she can escape, a Year Ten girl in tottering
heels slips on a dropped patch of Branston Pickle and

skids into us, swearing. A couple of Year Seven kids start yelling, and out of nowhere Buzz steps in to defend the girl in the heels.

It escalates quickly.

Lara's brother and his mates arrive in search of refreshment just in time to see Buzz threatening the Year Sevens with the punch ladle; there's lots of shouting and a full-on scrap breaks out. Lara's brother tells Buzz to leave, but Chris has joined him by then and they're not about to go without a fight.

In the background, the thudding sound of a punk playlist starts to pound out, which just ramps up the drama.

'I need to find my friend,' Eden repeats, but I hang on to her hand and pull her backwards, away from the scrum. Buzz has a bloody nose now, Chris is trying to smash Lara's brother over the head with his own guitar and the drunk girl in the heels lifts up the punch bowl and tips the entire contents on the kitchen floor.

'Sheesh. What's actually in that stuff?' Eden asks, horrified.

'You don't want to know,' I tell her. 'Let's get out of here.'

I find myself standing against a door with a notice taped

to it saying *'Private, Keep Out!'* I try the handle; it opens unexpectedly, and the two of us fall inside, laughing. I fumble for the light switch and discover we're in some kind of utility room.

Eden shuts the door and leans against it, eyes wide.

'Two years without one single party, and the first time I venture out I land up in the middle of a full-on fight,' she says. 'Just my luck!'

'Welcome to my world,' I say.

# 28

## Eden

I am sitting on the washing machine, squashed up against a pile of freshly laundered towels and a couple of bottles of fabric softener. Ryan Kelly is loafing in the laundry basket, one foot flexed against the utility room door to keep it shut, grinning. Outside in the kitchen, there is screaming, yelling, the sound of plates being smashed.

'Buzz and Chris are losers, seriously,' I say. 'There was no need for this!'

'They are,' Ryan agrees. 'Lovable losers, though. Sometimes. Well, occasionally, if I'm honest. And starting fights is what they do best!'

'Why do you hang around with them?' I ask.

Ryan shrugs. 'Things are never dull when Buzz and Chris are about, and they don't do deep and meaningful conversations, which is definitely a plus. They're a laugh – I don't have to think too much when I'm with them.'

I sip my cherryade. I'm not really in a position to criticize – at least Ryan has friends, even if they are of the bonehead variety.

'So you're friendly with Chloe, Flick and Ima now?' Ryan asks. 'That's cool.'

'I don't know them all that well, but they're nice,' I say.

I glance towards the laundry room door, guilt stricken. What if Andie is looking for me, if she finds me hiding away with Ryan? She's made it very clear that she is here to see me, after all, and not the others. Besides, she might not understand, and the last thing I want is to fall out with her again.

'Is that door locked?' I ask.

Ryan pushes his foot against it firmly and grins. 'Nobody can get in. OK?'

'OK,' I say. I am glad of that, and of course, the longer

we stay hidden the less chance there is of Ryan spotting Andie, and vice versa.

There's another crash outside, and I wince as someone or something thuds against the door. It looks like I'm stuck here for now; I hope Andie's OK too, and steering clear of the scrap.

'I'm glad you came,' Ryan is saying. 'It's good to see you out and about, having fun. You seem different tonight; more like the Eden I used to know. Why don't we ever speak these days, Eden? Hang out? What happened?'

I almost laugh out loud at this. 'You walked straight past me on the first day at Moreton Park,' I remind him. 'You didn't want to know me. You cut me dead, like you'd never seen me before. That's why we don't talk, Ryan. That's why we don't hang out.'

He hangs his head. 'Guilty as charged,' he admits. 'You want to know why? I didn't recognize you. You'd dyed your hair black and you looked all pale and sad. You were mooching along like you wanted to be invisible, and when you looked at me there was no spark, no recognition at all. I genuinely messed up, and once I'd blanked you I didn't know how to go back.'

'You could have said sorry,' I suggest. 'You could have explained . . .'

'What can I say?' Ryan tells me. 'I'm a loser, just like my so-called mates. I'm sorry, Eden.'

On the other side of the door, Lara is shouting that she's called the police. There's the sound of wood splintering, as if the kitchen chairs are being bashed to bits. To say that this party is not working out quite the way I hoped is the understatement of the year.

I look at Ryan, sad-faced, sprawled in the laundry basket, and sigh. How can I blame him for being messed up when I am just as bad?

'Doesn't matter,' I say. 'It's a long time ago now.'

Ryan scrambles up out of the laundry and stands in front of me, his face serious. The horrible skinhead cut he had back in Year Seven has grown out now and his hair is longer than it was when we were kids, dark waves springing back from his forehead. His grey eyes shine with a mixture of mischief and sadness, and he has razor-sharp cheekbones I have never noticed before. The tips of my ears are going pink again, I know it.

'It matters to me,' he says. 'I messed up, and I'm sorry.

But hey, we had fun tonight; dancing, sorting the laundry, swapping character assassinations. Let's be friends, Eden. It'd be crazy not to . . .'

'Friends,' I say faintly. 'Sure.'

Then he leans over and kisses my ear, just like he did two years ago, and panic floods through me. It's happening all over again, and it can't, it mustn't, not now. Not ever.

What am I even doing with Ryan when I should be with Andie? I have to find her, get her out of this place before everything falls to bits.

I push Ryan away and jump down from the washing machine, shove the laundry basket out of the way and drag the door open, then step outside and slam it shut again with Ryan inside. The kitchen looks like a tornado has just passed through, and partygoers are standing around looking shell-shocked. I pick my way through the debris of a smashed chair, a hail of broken glass, puddles of fruit punch and soggy pizza. Buzz is sitting in a corner, blood trickling from his nose,

'Eden!' Ryan is yelling behind me. 'Wait!'

But I don't wait – I can't. I have to keep the two of them apart. I step into the crowded hallway. Miraculously, through the chaos I see Andie talking into her mobile, lifting her hand up above the crowd to signal to me.

'Eden!' Andie yells over the screech of the amps, the thud of the bass. 'Look . . . bad timing; something's come up. I have to go!'

I try to yell back, but my shout is swallowed up by the squeal of a police siren outside. Instantly, the crowd turns and begins to push against me; everyone is trying to get back to the kitchen, possibly to the back door. Nobody wants to be caught underage drinking or accused of trashing the place. They are looking for a quick escape.

I feel sick. I try to elbow my way towards Andie, but it's like swimming against the tide. Why did I leave Andie? Why did I waste the little time we have together dancing and hiding out with Ryan?

Three police officers appear in the doorway and begin to push their way into the hall. They pass Andie without so much as a glance. Lara appears at my side, crying, telling the police officers that gatecrashers spiked the punch and picked a fight, and that her parents are going to kill her. I feel for her, but right now, no matter how much I may sympathize, I need to get to my best friend.

I'm panicking, pushed, shoved, sworn at.

I'm way, way too slow.

By the time I get to the doorway, Andie has gone.

## 29

## Ryan

I must have a very guilty face, because I have a hard job persuading the police that I had nothing to do with the vandalism. Eventually, Lara and her brother step in and say I was not involved, and the minute I'm off the hook I head off in search of Eden.

Chloe, Flick and Ima are outside, waiting for Flick's dad to pick them up.

'Eden left,' Chloe tells me. 'We told her to hang on, that Flick's dad would drop her home, but she wouldn't wait. She looked upset – what did you say to her, Ryan Kelly?'

'Nothing!' I protest.

'You'd better not have,' Ima threatens.

I wave to the girls and break into a run, following the route Eden was most likely to take, and I finally catch up with her by the park.

'Eden,' I say, catching hold of her wrist. 'Wait up! Where are you going?'

Her blue eyes slide right past me as if I'm not there.

'I'm going home,' she says, heading for the park gates. 'I shouldn't have come . . .'

'You can't just wander around in the dark on your own,' I argue. 'I'll walk you home, if that's where you're going. What's wrong?'

'Please, just go away!'

'Look, the park's not such a great idea,' I argue. 'Not in the dark, not on your own . . .'

'I'm not on my own, am I?' she counters, irritated. 'You're here. Why *are* you here again?'

'I'm being helpful,' I say.

'You're being a pain.'

'Tell me what's wrong, Eden,' I say. 'What happened? What did I do?'

'You think it's all about you, is that it?' she snaps. 'Well, get a grip, Ryan. The world doesn't revolve around you.

I've just had enough of the party, OK? Smashed up kitchens and police raids and hiding in cupboards is not my idea of fun.'

'It was fun, though, wasn't it?' I tease. 'Admit it!'

Her eyes flash with anger. 'Has anyone ever told you that you're the most annoying boy in the world?'

'Loads of people, all the time,' I admit. 'If you want to insult me, be original at least.'

'You're ridiculous!' she snaps. 'Idiotic, psychopathic, rebellious, stupid . . .'

'Don't hold back, now,' I say. 'Say what you think.'

'I will,' she replies, her voice shaking. 'You're throwing your life away, asking for trouble. It's like you actually enjoy being the school troublemaker.'

'Maybe I do.'

'Which proves my point,' Eden huffs. 'Idiotic. Stupid. And you're always sticking your nose in where it's not wanted. Why can't you get the message and just leave me alone?'

'Because I can't,' I say. 'I've tried, and I suppose I managed for a while, but the truth is I just can't. I care about you, Eden.'

'Nobody asked you to care!'

It's like watching the ice melt after a long, hard winter; the waters beneath are wild, dangerous, unpredictable. Eden's icy shell is falling away, but underneath there is chaos. Luckily, I like chaos a lot.

I shrug. 'Too bad,' I say. 'You don't get to decide whether I care or not, Eden. I just do. It's not a crime, y'know!'

'It just feels . . . wrong,' she says.

That makes me sad, because nothing has ever felt more right to me than being with Eden Banks.

## 30

## Eden

I can't hate Ryan, no matter how I try. We walk together to the children's playground, and I sit on the old wooden roundabout, curled up, face buried against my knees, hugging my legs. Ryan pushes the roundabout gently, then sits down on the segment next to me.

We don't talk for a long time; we just sit in the darkness as the roundabout spins slowly.

'I shouldn't have kissed your ear,' Ryan says eventually. 'It probably brought back bad memories, right? Of the camp-out sleepover . . . Andie's birthday. I didn't think.'

'You never do,' I tell him.

'You just have such irresistible ears, that's all,' he quips.

'I can't help myself. Look, Eden, would it help to talk about it?

'Not really,' I whisper, and my voice sounds like dry leaves, like grit and sawdust. 'Why start now? We never talk about stuff, Ryan. Not any more. Not for a long time.'

'Maybe it's time we started,' he says.

'I don't think I can,' I tell him honestly. 'Can't handle it. Can't talk about it. Can't even let myself think about it . . .'

'We're a mess, aren't we?' Ryan says with a sigh. 'It all went wrong. We should have handled it differently. We should have talked. Maybe we didn't try hard enough.'

I shrug. 'Maybe . . .'

'We're talking now, I guess,' he says. 'Better late than never. Seriously, I didn't mean to upset you.'

I shake my head. I feel empty, hollowed out, a husk of a person. There are no words I can find to properly explain the guilt I feel, or the shock I felt when Andie left. Ryan would never understand.

'Parties aren't my thing either, really,' he says, kicking at the ground again so the roundabout, almost at a standstill, picks up speed. 'All a bit crazy.'

He leans back, looking up at the stars. His hair is longer,

messier than it used to be, ruffled in the breeze. In the shadows he looks nothing like the Ryan I used to know, the boy who had my heart when I was eleven years old. Is he still the same boy inside?

'Buzz and Chris went way too far,' he is saying. 'They just can't help themselves. Spike the punch, pick a fight – it's what they do, but this time it backfired big time. I feel sorry for Lara. Teenage parties are way too dangerous; all those teenagers, all those hormones, all that music and expectation. Somehow or another, something is always going to go wrong. This is much better – you, me, a round-about in the park. If the excitement gets too much for us, we can always try the swings or the seesaw . . .'

'Not sure I could stand the thrill,' I say.

'Me neither . . .'

I smile sadly, uncurling a little to lean down and push the roundabout on.

'Parties and me are a bad, bad idea,' I say softly, settling back again. 'Seeing everyone from school . . . well, it made me remember how things used to be, before. Does that make sense?'

'It does to me,' he says. 'I guess . . . well, not everything is forever. That was a lesson we all had to learn. Things change. People change.'

'Did *you* change, Ryan?' I ask. 'Inside, I mean?'

'I don't think so,' he says. 'Underneath my teen criminal persona there still beats a heart of pure gold . . . just don't tell anyone. How about you?'

'I don't know,' I admit. 'I'm sort of scared to find out.'

He looks at me in the darkness, grey eyes serious. 'Don't be,' he says. 'Don't be scared to be you.'

Then he leans across and kisses me.

## 31

## **Ryan**

On the whole, it is a lot better kissing Eden's mouth than kissing her ear. Her lips taste of cherryade and sadness; her arms snake round my neck and pull me closer. The roundabout spins softly and my head drifts away, and when we finally draw apart we look at each other, wide-eyed, for the longest time.

I am just going in for a second kiss when she jumps down and races off into the darkness.

'Eden! Wait! I thought . . .'

'You didn't think at all,' she snaps. 'This can't happen! All the trouble it caused last time!'

'That was different,' I reason. 'We were kids then, Eden. OK, it caused some bad feeling.'

'It caused World War Three!' Eden yells. 'It was the end of everything!'

We're out of the park now and walking fast towards Eden's street. 'No, Eden, no; it was a silly, stupid row, that's all. We would have made up; everything would have been OK . . .'

'But we didn't, and it wasn't!' she says.

I try to put a hand on her arm, but she swats me away like I am some annoying insect.

'Eden,' I argue. 'Listen! That stuff at the camp-out sleepover; the ear kiss, the argument; it had nothing to do with what happened afterwards. You know that, don't you?'

She doesn't reply, just walks even faster, wiping her eyes again.

'Don't walk away, Eden,' I say. 'This is serious. Have you been feeling guilty all this time? Blaming yourself? Because what happened was bad enough without all that.'

We're at the top of Eden's street now, speeding down towards her flat. The houses are big Victorian semis, some filled with families, some divided into flats. Eden's flat is in one of the neater houses. A big apple tree arches over the wall in the front garden; as kids we used to pick all the apples the minute they appeared and eat them even though they were sour and hard, and we'd all get stomach ache. Who picks those apples now?

'Eden?' I prompt.

'Drop it, Ryan,' she says. 'I can't do this right now.'

'When can you do it, then? Tomorrow? Next week? Next year? I think we need to talk, Eden. Properly. There are things that need to be said.'

'It's a bit late for you to start caring now!'

'That's not fair,' I protest. 'I've always cared, you know that. Stop shutting everyone out – stop shutting *me* out!'

She opens the wrought-iron gate and slams it closed behind her, with me on the other side. She looks at me for a moment, her eyes smudged with blue shadow, her cheeks smeared with glitter; in the yellow light from the street lamp she looks more beautiful than ever.

'I'll call for you on Monday,' I say. 'You'll feel better by then.'

'Ryan,' she whispers. 'I just . . . can't.'

I hold my hands up, a gesture of surrender.

'Just friends,' I promise. 'No kisses, no hugs, no holding hands – no nothing, not unless you say so. OK?'

'Ryan, this won't work,' she says.

She runs along the path and I hear the click of a key in the big old front door, and no matter how hard I try I can't think of a single thing to stop her.

## 32

## Eden

I am going to be a hermit, possibly for the rest of my life. It's Monday and I'm still in bed at midday, festering under the duvet even though it's boiling outside. The curtains are tightly closed to keep out the prying sun.

The first time I lost Andie, it broke me. I knew I could never be the same again, so I didn't even try; I took refuge in sad songs, dark clothes, a stay-away stare to keep people at arm's length. I stumbled through life half asleep, my heart frozen, my soul numb.

This time, though . . . I really think that this time will kill me. It has been two days already without a word from

Andie. She said she'd be in touch. She promised, didn't she? Well, she said she'd try.

I've had a whole rash of text messages from Chloe, Flick and Ima, checking that I got home OK.

**My dad heard about the police raid**, Flick texted. **Now I'm grounded for the rest of the summer. How unfair is that? It was worth it, though. I have such a crush on Lara's brother! Don't tell anyone, OK?**

**Are you going out with Ryan Kelly now?** Chloe wanted to know. **He is such a weirdo, but quite cute too in a scary kind of way. And he is funny, I admit. Is it true his dog is half pit bull and half wolf?**

**Glad you got home safely**, Ima texted. **Wasn't the party awesome? I have never had so much fun. Shame it ended badly. I've gone off Branston Pickle for life. Lara said you were hiding in the utility room with Ryan Kelly – everybody's talking about it. Looks like you got hit with Cupid's javelin. Geddit? Arrow? Javelin? Oh, never mind!**

I bury my mobile under my pillow, too grumpy to even

think about replying, then dig it out again in case Andie calls. She doesn't.

There's a sudden sharp hail of gravel on glass, a sound I remember from long ago. Andie and Ryan went through a phase of refusing to use the doorbell; instead, they would throw gravel from the driveway at my bedroom window to grab my attention.

I'm out of bed in seconds, my heart pounding, but when I pull the curtains back it's just Ryan standing on the path with his ridiculous dog. Disappointment curdles in my belly.

Another bit of gravel hits the glass and I yank the window open.

'What are you doing?' I yell down. 'Go away, Ryan! I'm busy!'

'You're still in your pyjamas,' he points out. 'That's not what I would call *busy*.'

'Can't you take a hint, Ryan Kelly?' I call down, exasperated.

'Clearly not. I thought we had a date?'

'We do not have a date!' I tell him. 'I didn't agree to anything!'

Ryan just shrugs. 'Come down, Eden. I need your help,

and I'm happy to keep on shouting, but I think your neighbours might get hacked off.'

'Just go away, Ryan! Please?'

'Hey, I'm happy to wait,' he says. He sits down on the grass, opens a rucksack and takes out some kind of sandwich. Great. My front garden is some kind of public picnic ground now.

I slam the window shut and slouch to the bathroom to shower and dress. In the corner of my bedroom, the two piles of clothes Andie sorted lie untouched; part of me wants to pick something shapeless and grey from Andie's 'charity shop' pile, but I make myself choose scarlet jeans and a dark blue T-shirt. Dragging a comb through my hair, I stuff Ryan's paper crane into my jeans pocket and run down to the garden.

Ryan is stretched out on the grass beneath the apple tree, Rocket at his side. Ryan opens one eye and grins, as if I haven't just been yelling at him from my bedroom window.

'Cool!' he says, jumping to his feet. 'Let's get this show on the road!'

'Hang on, I haven't said I'm going anywhere . . .'

Rocket is leaping and jumping around me, pushing his

head against my hand, snuffling, huffing, looking for ice cream. I drop to my knees to fuss him properly, smiling at how Ryan's childhood doodles of his dream dog have turned into such perfect reality. Rocket is like every child's slightly wobbly drawing of their dream dog, with a personality to match.

'When did you get Rocket, then?' I ask, stroking the dog's ears. 'He is so perfect . . . just exactly what you imagined. I never thought your parents would cave in!'

'We got him from the dogs' home,' Ryan explains. 'He was three months old and he'd already been rehomed and brought back twice. I knew he was the one; who cares if other people thought he was difficult.'

'Was he?' I ask. 'Difficult?'

'Yeah, definitely, to start with. He howled all night, every night, for a week when we first got him. He peed so many times on the hall carpet we had to throw it out and get a new one. He ate my school bag and my gym shoes and my maths homework – well, I didn't mind about that, obviously. I took him to dog training classes but we got thrown out . . .'

'Because Rocket stole the dog treats and you got caught smoking,' I say. 'But you're OK now. You've stuck with him.'

'That's what you do, isn't it?' Ryan says. 'With stuff you care about. You stick around and keep trying, and eventually you come to an understanding. Badly behaved boy, badly behaved dog; we're a perfect match. We go running together, and that's cool. Play footy. And he has improved, loads. Although he did eat my mum's new high-heeled sandals last week.'

'Ouch,' I say. 'Bet that didn't go down well. How did you make her change her mind, anyway? She was always so dead set against dogs.'

'Trying to cheer me up,' he says with a shrug. 'After . . . well, you know.'

I do know, but I push the thought away. I stand up, arms folded, shoulders square. It's great what Ryan has achieved with Rocket, but he needs to know I am not some kind of project, someone to be rescued and rehabilitated. I do not want to be fixed up.

When people from my past show up, like Andie did last week, it creates nothing but trouble. I was safe, secure, almost invisible, but Andie somehow tricked me into chipping away at the ice-queen mask, digging beneath the surface to find myself again.

Look at how well *that* worked.

'Well,' I say. 'Nice of you to call, but like I said, I'm busy today. Busy for most of the holidays, in fact. OK? See you in September, maybe.'

'Nice try, Eden, but you don't shake me off that easily!'

Ryan fixes me with a steely, bright-eyed look and something flutters and flips over inside me. Two spots of pink burn in my cheeks, and everything I want to shout and yell and snarl at him dies on my lips.

'I made a picnic,' he says, cajoling.

'You've eaten most of it,' I argue.

'Eden, I need your help . . . please?'

'What with?'

'I'll show you,' he promises. 'C'mon!'

He takes my hand and my traitorous fingers tighten around his as if this was what they were waiting for.

'You said no hand-holding,' I remind him.

'I've changed the rules,' he says. 'Hand-holding but no kissing, OK? You get to call the shots.'

My feet fall into step with his and we head out of the garden, Rocket at our heels.

## 33

## **Ryan**

Showing Eden the garden at Miss Smith's place is cool. She looks around, wide-eyed and curious, full of challenges and ideas.

'No way,' she says, when she works out where we are. 'This is where you harpooned the old lady?'

'It was a javelin,' I correct her. 'And the old lady wasn't even outside at the time. Nobody got hurt. It was an accident . . . sort of!'

Eden frowns. 'The school grapevine says that javelin speared three fish, smashed a greenhouse and took the old lady's hat off. I heard someone say she fainted and had to have the paramedics round . . .'

'Rubbish,' I argue. 'There are no fish in the pond, and there's no greenhouse at all, smashed or otherwise. No hats or paramedics were involved.'

'I hate it, the whole rumour-mill at school,' she says. 'People will say anything if they think it makes a good story. I wonder what they say about me?'

'Beautiful, sad-eyed girl takes pity on school loser,' I quip. 'Hauls him back from off the rails and on to the straight and narrow . . .'

'I can't even rescue myself,' she says. 'Seriously. I am not a rescuer. Don't get your hopes up.'

I tell her about my plan to make amends for the javelin disaster by tidying up Miss Smith's garden, how I've already weeded and planted and strimmed, and how I'm going to mow the lawn today. We ring the doorbell and Miss Smith appears.

'Peter!' she exclaims, beaming. 'And Patch! Who's this you've brought to meet me? A lady friend? How exciting! What's your name, dear?'

'Eden.'

'Edie?' Miss Smith echoes, offering a wrinkled claw to

shake. 'That's a beautiful name. Well, you're very welcome! Any friend of Peter's is a friend of mine!'

'Who's Peter?' Eden whispers. 'What's going on?'

'She gets a bit muddled,' I say under my breath. 'She thinks I'm someone else; she thinks Rocket is someone else, too. She seems happy about it, though . . .'

Miss Smith gives me the key for the shed and I open it and drag out the ancient, rust-caked mower. It's a basic push-along one that looks like it could date from the reign of Queen Victoria, and from the state of the garden I'd guess it probably hasn't been used in a hundred years, either. OK, I may be exaggerating a little, but not much. I have to rub the thing down with wire wool and wipe it with oil and twiddle with it a bit, but after a while I manage to get it moving.

While I'm doing this Eden unearths a slightly mildewed deckchair and sets it up beside the back door. She is braver than me, and ventures into the house to find a pale blue knitted shawl to cover the stains and a cushion to make it more comfortable, then sets up Miss Smith in the sunshine with a glass of ice-cool orange squash and a couple of cheese sandwiches from the picnic rucksack.

'Lovely, dear,' she says, and Eden grins. When she does that, it's like sunshine through clouds; it lights up everything and makes the world sparkle.

By the time I've finished mowing, Eden has rigged up a sunshade to keep the old lady from getting sunburnt, and Rocket is stretched out on the path at Miss Smith's feet.

'Peter will tell you, this pond was lovely once,' Miss Smith is telling Eden. 'Big orange goldfish, we had, and water lilies. Dragonflies used to come in the summer – their wings were like tiny rainbows!'

'Wow,' Eden says. 'I'd love to have seen that!'

She rolls up her jeans and wades into the pond, her arms speckled with mud as she uproots reeds, skimming off skeins of pondweed with a long stick.

I wander over and poke at the ancient blue pond liner with a finger, watching it crumble and split. 'Don't go getting any big ideas about fixing up the pond,' I say. 'This liner must be decades old! We can tidy it up a bit, pull out the weed, but it's never going to hold enough water for goldfish'

Eden frowns. 'New liner, then?' she says. 'I really think we can make it beautiful again, Ryan. C'mon, we have to try!'

I can't help grinning because she said 'we'. I like the sound of that. I'm also smiling because it's the first time in ages I have seen Eden sounding excited about something, even if that something is just an overgrown garden. So what? If she wants to buy a water lily and some goldfish, we'll do it.

Eden is wrong about not being a rescuer.

She has Miss Smith sitting in the sun, eating and drinking, which is kind of awesome, and by the time we're ready to leave, the old lady is looking happier and more alert than I've ever seen her.

'Come again, Edie,' she says. 'And look after my Peter, won't you? He's a good boy!'

I wink and stick my tongue out, and Eden laughs.

## 34

## Eden

The two of us make plans to buy goldfish and a new pond liner from a big garden centre on the edge of town, and I head for home with a spring in my step.

I decide to surprise Mum with a chocolate fridge cake, and once I'm in the kitchen smashing up digestive biscuits and melting chocolate and stirring in fruit, I remember why I loved baking so much. Maybe I'll try something more ambitious next time? Mum is pleased, anyhow, and we eat a slice each after tea, watching a slushy DVD and sipping orange juice with ice. My mobile buzzes halfway though, but it's just Ryan reminding me where to meet next day.

**Operation Goldfish: eleven o'clock at the bus stop by the park gates**, he says. **Don't be late!**

**Wouldn't dare**, I text back, grinning.

'A friend?' Mum asks, looking up from the DVD. 'That's nice!'

'Yeah . . . a friend,' I say, hiding a smile.

I'm still smiling as I set out faded denim shorts and a pale blue T-shirt for tomorrow, choosing from the dwindling pile of clothes that Andie declared were OK. It's not that I am especially worried about how I look for Ryan – well, maybe a bit – but also that Andie's home truths have made me look at my clothes in a new light. Do I want to hide away in layers of anonymous grey-black? Part of me does, but another part is brave enough to say I've had enough of pretending to be someone I'm not. And if I'm not a Goth, isn't it time to work out exactly what and who I really am?

I think a shopping trip might be required, and wish that Andie was still around to come. Maybe Mum would go with me. She is always nagging me to get a bit of colour into my wardrobe.

As for the towering pile of baggy black combats and

outsize T-shirts and hoodies, I sigh and start packing them into carrier bags to take to the charity shop. I'm just finishing the third bag when my mobile bleeps, and I pick it up, expecting another message from Ryan.

A different name flashes up: Andie.

My heart races as I click on the message.

**Sorry I had to leave in such a hurry on Friday**, it says. **Something came up. Looks like the party ended with a bit of a bang! I noticed Ryan was there – did you talk to him? A little bird told me the two of you were getting on great! ((oxox))**

I throw my mobile on the bed, hands shaking. Once upon a time Andie and I texted maybe twenty, thirty times a day. We texted every minute we weren't together, sharing the slightest thoughts, the smallest things. We held a mirror up to each other's lives.

It's been two years now since I've had a text from my best friend; two years is a long time. Even when she was around last week, she didn't text, just came and went when it suited her.

Something came up? What does that even mean? And what does she mean about Ryan? Did she see us? Is she angry? How does she know? I think of Andie's birthday sleepover and the fight that followed, and for a moment I panic. It takes a moment for my breath to slow again, and when it does I pick the phone up and type out a reply.

**Miss you so, so much, Andie. I wish you'd waited a minute so we could say a proper goodbye. How do you know about Ryan? xxx**

The answer appears almost at once.

**Aha, I know all sorts of things, Eden! You're my best friend, right? It's my job! Well, actually I saw you both dancing to the band – looked like you were having fun! Be nice to Ryan . . . he's had a hard time. Sorry again I had to leave so fast; it was a bit of an emergency. Speak soon! oxox**

Ryan's had a hard time? What about me? And what kind of best friend vanishes for two years and then turns up again as though nothing has happened? I don't care, I realize. Where Andie is concerned, I will forgive anything. Exasperated, I text back to tell her that I'm seeing Ryan tomorrow, that I'm biting the bullet, taking the clothes she sorted to the charity shop. I even get brave and ask her when she might be in town again.

There's no reply. My phone stays silent all evening.

Hearing from Andie again stirs up all kinds of confusing thoughts; things I don't even want to think about. Is this how it will be from now on? A couple of brief text messages now and then, so that she can check up on me, make believe we are still best mates? It's not enough. I don't want to be best friends with a girl who is never around, not any more. I touch the broken heart necklace; the silver pendant lies cool and heavy against my collarbone.

It wasn't just the Heart Club that broke when Andie went away, it was my own heart, too, and I am weary of holding myself together. It was getting harder and harder, and then Andie came back and started chipping away at the shell I'd built around myself. She told me she knew what she was doing, that it was all for the best, but then she vanished and I was lost all over again.

I still haven't worked out whether the kiss has made things better or worse. Maybe it was just the last straw, getting under my skin when my defences were down, waking up my feelings again after two years in the deep freeze. I feel like Sleeping Beauty in the fairy story, with Ryan as the handsome prince who has to hack his way through a thorn forest armed only with a javelin. I'm not beautiful, of course, but Ryan could pass for handsome and I am starting to see that his bad boy persona is just as much a mask, an act, as my ice maiden one has been.

We are both damaged goods, Ryan and me.

Is there hope for the two of us? I have no idea, but here I am, the blue spotty scarf from Friday night tied up in my hair, a swipe of eyeliner and a smudge of shadow accenting my eyes like Andie showed me. I dawdle through the park, checking my mobile for the time, knowing I'm going to be way too early for our meeting.

Ryan has texted three times already this morning, reminding me of the time, the rendezvous, asking me to bring a bucket to carry home the fish. He seems keen, but what are we to each other really? Strangers, friends, something more? How am I supposed to tell?

Is this a date or just a goldfish expedition, a pond renovating afternoon – even just some kind of weird voluntary service exercise in aid of lonely elderly ladies? Does it matter?

I have named the fish in my head already; Fish and Chips. I wonder if the names will make Ryan laugh, if I'll dare to tell him.

I drag my feet, loiter at the playground, buy an ice cream from the van and sit on a bench to eat it all, being extra careful not to drip anything on my clothes. All that and I am still ten minutes early, but when I come out of the park gates it doesn't matter because Ryan is at the bus stop already, checking his mobile, brushing down his jeans, straightening his T-shirt.

Then he sees me and his eyes light up and my heart feels like it's lifting up, right out of me, like a bird in flight.

I'm not scared any more. My heart's already broken, so the worst that can happen is that he might break another little piece of it. And maybe that won't happen. Maybe.

## 35

## **Ryan**

Today I wake up happy for the fourth day running. It could be the sunshine, or the school holidays. Alternatively, it could be Eden.

She is like a chrysalis turning slowly into a butterfly, breaking free of the shell that has cocooned her for the past two years. She's fragile still, uncertain, but if I step back and let her stretch her wings, she might just come back to me. I am hopeful.

Me? I might be changing too, slowly. Who knew?

Buzz and Chris have been texting, asking me to come and hang out in the shopping centre in town. Buzz has worked out that you can stand up on the gallery level and drop water bombs on the shoppers, then make a quick getaway through the multistorey car park.

**It doesn't hurt them or anything**, he texts. **It's just balloons filled with water. A bit of water never hurt anyone, did it? It'll be a right laugh!**

**Busy**, I text back, and switch off my mobile.

I wonder why I ever thought that Buzz and Chris were funny, because lately they are bugging me big style. What if people see me the way they see Buzz and Chris? Clumsy, careless, crass? Not funny, but scary, annoying, embarrassing? The thought of that makes me feel very bad indeed.

Eden and I sit on the top deck of the number 23 bus heading out of town, talking about pond liners and gold-fish. It shouldn't be romantic but it kind of is. Technically we're just friends working on a project together to make life a little bit nicer for a lonely old lady, but both of us know it's more than that. We pretend not to care. We don't hold hands – we barely touch at all – but the air around us feels electric.

A couple of times yesterday, I looked up and caught Eden looking at me, and my cheeks darkened with colour like they did when I was six years old. It's like having a fever – that hectic, heightened way you feel when you're about to get ill with flu or something.

'When we've done the pond, we'll have to have a look at that frazzled old tree,' Eden says now. 'And we can paint the fence so it's not horrible bare wood. Cool, right?'

'Cool,' I say.

'We could make a hammock, too,' she suggests. 'Is Miss Smith too old for hammocks, d'you think?'

'Nobody's too old for a hammock,' I say breezily, even though I know Miss Smith probably couldn't even walk as far as the trees, let alone kick back in a hammock. She is more a Zimmer-frame kind of girl, to be fair.

'I'm going to bake her cookies,' Eden decides. 'Shortbread ones. Or macaroons. Old-fashioned ones, anyway. I'll put them in a tin, with a paper doily underneath. She'll like that. Have you noticed she calls me Edie – isn't that cute?'

'You are kind of cute,' I tease, and Eden digs me with an elbow.

'Shhh,' she says. 'This is serious!'

It's serious, all right. I am a lost cause, a hopeless case. I grin.

'Miss Smith thinks your name is Peter and that Rocket's name is Patch,' she points out. 'Who d'you think the real Peter is? A neighbour? A grandson?'

'A neighbour, maybe,' I say. 'From the past. She never married, so it can't be a grandson. Whoever it is, I bet he's all grown-up and gone to uni by now. As for Patch . . .'

'Aw, don't,' she says. 'Poor Patch. Probably long gone. Poor Miss Smith; d'you think anyone ever visits her, apart from us?'

I shrug. 'Never seen anyone.'

'It sucks to be lonely,' Eden says, and I get the feeling she knows what she's talking about. I guess we both do.

# 36

## Eden

We have a trolley with folded-up pond liner in it, and a water lily, and water irises. We also have two small goldfish swimming in circles in the plastic bucket. They are a lot smaller than planned; we didn't have enough money for the big kind.

'Fish and Chips,' I say, watching them flick their tails as we queue for Coke floats in the garden centre cafe. 'Aren't they beautiful?'

'Hope they're worth it,' Ryan retorts. 'D'you think Miss Smith will even notice?'

'Of course she will,' I say. 'She'll love them!'

We sit down at an outside table with the Coke floats.

'We are co-owners of two small goldfish,' Ryan says. 'Does that make us foster parents? Do we take it in turns to feed them, in case Miss Smith forgets?'

'Once term starts, we can do it on the way home from school,' I say. 'Not a problem. I've always wanted a pet, and we're not allowed them at the flat. It's a win-win situation!'

At that moment, a little girl in the distinctive green blazer and tartan skirt of St Bernadette's comes into the cafe with her mum; they pick out cakes and drinks, and I catch little wisps of their conversation.

'So glad you enjoyed the induction morning . . . great opportunity to mix with your new classmates . . . what did you think of the Latin taster class? Latin opens so many doors . . .'

'This blazer is *boiling*,' the little girl says as she passes our table. 'Roll on winter!'

'I can offer you a half-share in Rocket, if you like,' Ryan is saying. 'He already likes you better than me. You gave him ice cream . . .'

I nudge his arm and nod towards the little girl.

'Look,' I whisper. 'She's been to one of those induction

216

mornings at St Bernadette's. Remember when Hasmita had to do that? It seems like so long ago!'

'Scary uniform,' Ryan says with a frown. 'This is the twenty-first century – who wears tan-coloured tights these days? And that skirt; green, orange and yellow tartan? Nasty.'

The two of them wander off to a table across the court-yard, out of earshot, and I sigh.

'I hated that,' I say. 'When Hasmita kept vanishing off to induction mornings and we started to realize that she wasn't going to be around any more.'

'I know,' Ryan says. 'The beginning of the end.'

My eyes follow the little girl and her mum.

'Do you ever see Hasmita?' I ask. 'It seems crazy that she's here, in the very same town as us, and yet we never speak. At least, I don't . . .'

'Me neither,' Ryan admits. 'Nor Tasha. I tried emailing her, just after they went, but I never got a reply.'

'Snap,' I say. 'I saw Hasmita in town not long ago, and she cut me dead.'

'Ouch,' Ryan says.

'I know. This probably sounds mad, but . . . well, I was

thinking maybe I might try again. Write a letter to Tasha, perhaps. Call and see Hasmita. Try to make contact. Is that a crazy idea?'

Ryan smiles. 'Not crazy,' he says. 'It's a good idea. But . . . be careful, Eden. Some broken things can't be put back together, no matter how hard you try.'

## 37

# Ryan

I've spent so much time trying to forget that summer – the one between Year Six and Year Seven, but suddenly it's there in my mind as clearly as if it happened yesterday. How we started to fall apart.

Tasha's parents had sold their house and they threw a big farewell party. Everybody went. The adults drank too much wine and everyone promised to keep in touch, visit often, book the holiday cottage for summer forays to France. Those promises weren't kept in the end, obviously. The camp-out sleepover had been our last chance to be together as the Heart Club, but of course, that was where everything went into meltdown.

Things could have been so different. If it hadn't been raining, if Eden hadn't twisted her ankle dancing on the muddy grass, if I hadn't helped her back to the tent and kissed her ear. And even then – even then – it could still have been OK if only Andie hadn't seen us.

I'd been shell-shocked, horrified. I don't think I'd really understood until that moment that Andie hadn't been prac- tising her flirting on me at all; she'd been deadly serious.

'How could you?' she said to us, her voice like ice. 'How could you *do* that to me?'

Eden's face was a pale mask of hurt in the moonlight, tears running down her cheeks like rain.

'Please, Andie,' she said. 'It didn't mean anything, I swear. I don't want anything to come between us, not ever – please!'

None of us had ever seen Andie act this way. She was usually easy-going, happy, fun. Sure, she liked to be the centre of attention, but none of us had seen this mean streak before.

'Blame me,' I cut in. 'Eden slipped and I was trying to help her, and I just thought it would be funny to –'

'Funny?' Andie yelled. 'You thought it would be funny?

To kiss Eden? Yeah, I can see how kissing her must be a bit of a joke.'

'That's not what I meant,' I argued, but nobody was listening to me by then. Hasmita was wiping Eden's tears and Tasha was trying to calm Andie down, but neither of them were getting very far.

'Shh, shh,' Tash whispered. 'You don't mean it, Andie, you know you don't.'

'Of course I mean it!' Andie raged. 'Don't you even get it? This is my *birthday*! My special day, and you've ruined it, all of you. I can't believe you could do this to me, today of all days. You're supposed to be my friends! Did you plan it? Were you laughing behind my back all this time? Were you in on the joke too, Tasha? Hasmita? Oh, God, you must hate me so much.'

'No way!' Hasmita protested. 'We didn't know a thing!'

'There wasn't anything to know,' I argued. 'You're out of order, Andie! Get a grip!'

But like I said, nobody was listening to me by then.

'We didn't plan anything!' Eden said, stricken. 'You've got this all wrong, Andie! I *am* your friend. I could never hate you, never!'

Andie's eyes blazed. 'Too bad,' she snarled. 'Because I hate you! Get away from me, Eden Banks – I never want to see you again!'

I didn't know how to stop the meltdown. When boys fight, it's much simpler; someone gets upset, and you fight about it until one person wins, and then you put it all behind you. This was way more complicated, and I was out of my depth.

'Your mum's coming to get you,' I said to Eden. 'I'll wait with you. This will all blow over, you'll see, and Andie will calm down.'

'I will not calm down!' Andie snapped. 'Just go away, Ryan!'

'Eden?' I said, and she turned on me, eyes dark with anger.

'Go away, Ryan,' she spat. 'Like Andie said, haven't you done enough damage? This is all your fault!'

Andie vented her anger on Eden and Eden turned on me, pushing me away, blaming me for everything.

Seriously, it was bad. World War Three erupted, and the rest is history.

The camp-out sleepover; that was when the cracks in our friendship had finally grown too big. We fell apart, and nobody even tried to put us together again.

## 38

## Eden

The new pond looks amazing. We spent all day at Miss Smith's, pulling the old one apart, digging a deeper hole and lowering in the pond liner. We edged the pond with big stones and boulders and used the hosepipe to fill it up before planting water irises along the edges. We let the little plastic basket containing the water lily sink slowly down to the bottom of the pond. Finally, once the sun had warmed the water, we lowered the bucket with Fish and Chips and watched them swim free.

'Let's show Miss Smith!' I said, splashing out of the pond and across the grass. The old lady was sitting in her deck-chair beneath the sunshade, the moth-eaten pale-blue shawl wrapped round her shoulders, a glass of orange squash and some broken Rich Tea biscuits on her lap. Rocket was curled at her feet, enjoying the shade, the strokes and a plentiful supply of biscuit crumbs.

It took ages to lead Miss Smith to the pond, with me and Ryan on either side of her. Her eyes misted with tears as she watched the fish streak through the water.

'We've called them Fish and Chips,' Ryan said. 'D'you like them? D'you like the pond?'

'Oh, yes . . . I do love Fish and Chips,' she said, but I think she was having a confused day and thinking of her dinner. 'Thank you Peter; thank you, Edie! I will so miss seeing you!'

'We'll keep on visiting,' Ryan promised rashly. 'Feed the fish. Cut the grass. Fill up the bird feeder. Don't worry!'

Underneath the bad-boy exterior, Ryan is still the coolest, kindest boy I know.

Now I am home and sitting cross-legged on my bed making paper cranes. My mobile buzzes with an incoming message; I expect it to be Ryan suggesting a fence-painting expedition, but when I swipe my mobile to see the message, my mouth goes dry.

Not Ryan. Andie.

**Thinking about you lots just now. So sad you lost touch with Tasha and Hasmita. I bet they miss you just as much as I do. I'd love to see the old gang together again and if anyone can make that happen, you can, Eden. Please? For old times' sake? Love you loads oxox**

My fingers shake as I let the phone drop on to the duvet, into a flock of perfectly folded paper cranes, rainbow bright.

Why me? Andie is the only one who could pull us all back together, surely? She knows I've tried and failed.

But she also seems to know that it's been on my mind all week.

**What if they don't want to know me?** I text back, and the reply is there almost instantly.

**Oh, Eden, how could you ever think that? Please try. Please? For me.**

After we fell apart, did I try hard enough to stay in touch with the others? Maybe not. The silence from

226

Tasha knocked my confidence, and Hasmita distanced herself just as clearly. She started at St Bernadette's and that was that; our friendship was over. I waited for her to text, to call, to come round to the house, but none of those things happened. Instead I sent her a text, bright and brave and not too needy, asking if she wanted to meet up one weekend.

**I'm a bit tied up for the next few weeks**, she texted back. **School's really full-on. I have to work hard just to keep up – I can't let Mum and Dad down, not after they've paid out all that money for me.**

**It might do you good to have some downtime**, I'd texted back. **Please?**

My phone was silent, and then a reply buzzed in.

**I'm busy this weekend. One of the girls from school is having a sleepover, and I have to go. I have to fit in, make new friends. You understand, don't you, Eden? I'll give you a call, OK?**

It wasn't OK. It felt like nothing would ever be OK again, and I didn't understand. How could Hasmita draw a line under the past and start all over again? How could she do it when I couldn't?

She didn't give me a call. She didn't text or email or contact me at all.

If I ever saw her in town, in her new bottle-green uniform with her new friends, I'd feel my own face freeze, my heart sink to the bottom of my Converse trainers. After a while, we stopped even pretending to say hello, until that painfully embarrassing encounter the other week, of course.

I'd like to see Hasmita again, tell her I am not a nobody.

As for Ryan, I've spent a whole two years pretending he didn't exist.

Crossed wires, clumsy mistakes; a catalogue of errors only now being put right. What if I got things wrong with Tasha and Hasmita, too?

I have my friendship with Ryan back – could I reach out to the others as well?

I emailed Tash a few times, two years ago; she didn't answer, and those emails are lost now. We changed our provider eighteen months ago, got new addresses. What if Tash had tried to answer since then? I pick my old address book off the shelf; it's a spiral bound book with a Hello Kitty motif. Inside, under T for Tasha, I find my old friend's childhood address, a line scored through it, and her new address in France, written in her childish, curling handwriting, the night of the garden sleepover.

I emailed Tasha, sure, but I didn't actually write a letter. Maybe it's time to try?

I find some typing paper and a fineliner pen, take a deep breath. The letter starts off awkward and stilted, but after a while I get into it. I ask about life in France, about school and friends and boys, about how she is coping with the language. I tell her I am hopeless at French.

*Maybe,* I write, *I could write to you in French, and you can write back, and we can help each other?*

Maybe.

I give Tasha my email address, my Instagram, my mobile, my phone number. I tell her I miss her, need her, think of her every day. And then I fold the pages up and slide them into an envelope, copy out the address and find some stamps. It costs more to post a letter overseas, but I'm not sure how much more, so I stick on three stamps to be on the safe side.

I walk to the pillar box on the corner and post the letter before I can change my mind.

After that, there's nothing left to do but hope.

# 39

# Ryan

I learned all my coolest stuff from Andie. She was the girl next door, the girl everyone loved, the girl who was always at the centre of everything. She used to lean over the fence and yell my name, ask if I wanted to invent a new language or draw a map of the woods or hire a boat to go out on the park lake, pretending we were visiting Acapulco, Mexico City, the Galapagos Islands.

Pond digging? Trips to the garden centre? Andie would not have been impressed with that. I decide to raise the stakes.

I arrange to meet Eden at the park at one, down by the lake, and by the time she arrives I've set out a picnic rug and unpacked cold pizza, sandwiches, apples and iced buns from the bakery. A bottle of lemonade is wedged into the shallows of the boating lake, blocked in with a couple of boulders.

Eden turns up in frayed shorts and a stripy top, her arms and legs brown from our pond-digging project; the minute she sees the picnic she starts to laugh, and I can't help thinking that she looks worlds away from the pale, sad-faced girl who mooched along the school corridors wearing her pain on her sleeve like a badge of honour.

'No Rocket today?' she asks.

'He'd have stolen the picnic,' I say. 'He'd have chewed the rug, chased the squirrels, jumped in the lake and then shaken himself dry all over us. Nope, no Rocket today. He can have the leftovers, maybe!'

'It's so cool, Ryan,' she says. 'I love it!'

We flop down on the rug and start to eat, chatting idly about Miss Smith and the new goldfish.

'She has probably forgotten they're even there,' Eden says, frowning. 'Or that we've actually done anything. I reckon she slips back and forward in time – lives in the past, y'know? And I'd still love to know who she thinks we actually are. She kept calling you a good boy; clearly a case of mistaken identity!'

'Oi, you! But yes, we'll have to keep an eye on the pond,' I say, unwilling to accept that the project is at an end. 'We can go every few days to feed Fish and Chips, check they're OK.'

'Every day might be better,' she replies. 'To start with, at least. Until we're sure they've settled.'

I grin. How do you tell if a fish has 'settled'? It could take a while.

'We could paint the fence next week,' I suggest. 'While we're there.'

Suddenly, a football lands smack in the middle of our picnic, splattering everything, and I look up to see Buzz and Chris running across the grass towards us. I groan, mortified.

'Hey, lovebirds!' Buzz snorts, skidding to a halt beside us. 'What's this? Romantic picnics in the park, Ryan? Blowing out your mates to get mushy with some mystery chick?'

'This is Eden Banks,' I say, because my mates clearly haven't made the connection. 'From school.'

'Charmed, I'm sure,' Buzz says, holding out a hand to

shake and then making a loud burping noise the minute Eden is foolish enough to take it. 'Oops!'

'You didn't show at the shopping mall,' Chris says. 'Better things to do, huh? You missed a right laugh! Although we did get caught and cautioned by the security guards.'

'Got any cute friends?' Buzz is asking Eden. 'You could fix us up with a couple of cool chicks.'

She just rolls her eyes.

'Look, Ryan, how about you ditch all this slushy stuff and come play footy?' Chris says. 'You've been really boring this holidays. You should hang out with your mates sometimes, or you might find they've moved on without you!'

'Is that a promise?' I say.

Buzz grabs a handful of pizza slices and takes a bite from three of them at once. 'You're making a big mistake, mate,' he says. 'Just don't come crawling to me when she leaves you high and dry! See you around!'

The two of them amble away, scanning round for more mischief as they go.

'They're not happy with you,' Eden comments.

'Do I look like I care?' I say. 'I'm not sure what I ever saw in those idiots.'

'Trouble,' she says. 'Looks like we've both made some mistakes, Ryan, but I'm glad we're friends again, I really am. I've got a confession. I wrote a letter to Tasha last night. I don't know if she'll answer – she might just ignore it, like she did my emails – but still, I'm glad I did it. Has to be worth another try, right?'

I raise an eyebrow. 'Sure; that's brilliant!' I say. 'Maybe I'll try again, too.'

She flashes me a smile. 'Cool. Next I'm going to get really brave and call to see Hasmita. What's the worst that can happen? She might blank me again, but at least I'll know I've tried.'

'Want me to come with you?' I offer.

Eden leans back on the picnic rug, thoughtful. 'No, I think it's something I need to do alone; something I should have done ages ago. Clear the air. But thanks, Ryan. I'll tell you know how it goes!'

40

## Eden

I used to know Hasmita's house inside out, but it looks different now, the small front lawn paved over and the old front door with its slightly peeling paint replaced with one of those modern things made of fancy plastic and double-glazed glass. It seems colder, less welcoming than I remember.

I take a deep breath and walk along the path, push the doorbell.

Hasmita's mum opens the door, her eyes opening wide at the sight of me.

'Oh! Hello, Eden,' she says. 'What a lovely surprise!'

Hasmita appears in the hallway. Half a dozen different

expressions flit across her face, all in the space of a few seconds. Shock, guilt, sadness, panic . . . those are just some of them. Is she glad to see me, underneath? I can't even begin to tell.

'Hey,' I say. 'Long time no see.'

'Too right,' she replies. 'Look . . . you'd better come in.'

Hasmita pours us orange juice and finds cookies in the cupboard; we take them up to her room. It is tidier than the last time I was here, the Disney princess posters banished, replaced with pin-ups of some dodgy boy-band that Chloe, Flick and Ima also like. She puts on a Taylor Swift CD we'd once loved, and we chat in an awkward, stilted way about schools, uniforms, teachers, homework; anything except what's really on our minds.

'You dropped the Goth look,' Hasmita says, stating the obvious. 'You look more like you again.'

'Not so much of a nobody any more?' I quip.

'About that,' she says. 'I'm really sorry; you weren't meant to hear. I mean, that's no excuse, I know. I didn't mean it the way it sounded. I just didn't want to go into the whole story with Jen and Lisa, you know?'

I do know, I suppose, and I try to smile at Hasmita to

show there are no hard feelings, but I don't quite manage it and the conversation dies again. When I find myself mentioning the heatwave and how hot it's been lately, I know I am scraping the barrel. It's August, after all. Warm weather is hardly big news. Finally I run out of ideas and the conversation fizzles completely. The two of us have never been stuck for words before. At sleepovers, her mum used to have to knock on the bedroom door at three in the morning to get the lot of us to shut up, but those days are very clearly gone.

I wish I'd never come. Whatever friendship there might have been between Hasmita and me, it is over.

I put my glass down, make an excuse and stand up. I tried, at least, but I've left it way too late. The bond we once shared is broken now, dust and ashes.

I'm about to leave when Hasmita grabs my arm.

'I'm sorry,' she blurts. 'Please don't go, not yet! I'm so sorry, Eden. I've been a terrible, terrible friend.'

What am I supposed to say to that?

I don't have to say anything, though, because Hasmita is still talking. 'I just got it wrong. I tried to block out what happened, pretend everything was still OK. The easiest way to do that was to start over, and that's exactly what I did. I started at St Bernadette's; a brand-new beginning. I didn't want to think about the Heart Club, about any of it, and that meant dropping you and Ryan and Tasha as well. I just wanted it all to go away.'

'I guess we all did,' I admit.

Hasmita looks at me, her eyeliner smudged and blotchy, her lashes damp with tears. 'I'm sorry I pretended I didn't know you the other week,' she says. 'I feel so bad about that, but I knew I couldn't talk to you, couldn't talk about . . . well, what happened. You know?'

'I know,' I say. 'It was my fault, too.'

'None of it has worked, though,' Hasmita is saying. 'Not for me. You can't forget it, you can't run away from it and there's nobody else who really understands!'

I put an arm around Hasmita, stroke her long, dark hair.

'Shhh,' I whisper. 'I understand, OK? And I've made those mistakes too, believe me. It doesn't matter, now. None of it does.'

Suddenly, it doesn't. We talk for a long time, Hasmita and me. We talk about the old days, about Andie and Ryan and Tasha. It's like picking our way through a minefield, because there are still lots of things we can't say, don't say – not yet, anyhow. But it's a start.

Hasmita hasn't even tried to email Tasha – not once – and that shocks me because the two of them were once as close as Andie and me. I guess it helps to see that I'm not the only person hurting here, the only person who's messed up. It's all of us.

'Can you forgive me?' Hasmita asks. 'Please, Eden? I got it all so wrong; maybe we both did. I've missed you!'

'I've missed you too!'

I tell her about my attempts to change, to become invisible.

'The dyed hair and the black baggy clothes,' she says. 'I wondered what that was about. I'm glad you went back to your real colour; it suits you loads better.'

I almost tell her that Andie thinks so too, but think better of it. Andie was very clear that she wasn't ready to meet the others, and that might hurt Hasmita's feelings.

'It just feels like I'm starting to be me again,' I say instead. 'I have bags of old stuff to take to the charity shop, though. Whatever happens, I'm not going to hide any more. I'm fed up with being invisible. I need to go shopping for some stuff that isn't all grey and gloomy, so if you're ever at a loose end . . .'

'I'll come shopping with you!' she says at once. 'You know I will! I'd love to. And I am still the makeover queen, trust me. Actually, I saw a cute little pinafore dress in Topshop last week – not my thing, but totally you, Eden. And they have some brilliant T-shirts; I can be your stylist!'

'You can!' I promise. 'Next week? I've got money saved up and Mum will probably give me something, too!'

Hasmita's eyes shine.

'Are we friends again, Eden?' she asks, hopeful.

'We've never not been friends,' I tell her. 'We've just been . . . lost.'

## 41

# Ryan

We make another trip to see Miss Smith, and this time we paint the six-foot fence with soft yellow emulsion paint. It isn't the right kind of paint, and we haven't primed the wood or sanded it or anything, but my cash has run out and there's a big tin of yellow paint in the shed, ancient and lumpy and thick as custard, but still usable. Just. It seems like the right thing to do.

I mix up the paint and pour half into an old enamel saucepan (also from the shed) and clean up two ancient, cobwebby brushes. Eden and I start at opposite ends of the fence and paint towards each other, and when we meet in the middle she reaches out with one paint-spattered finger and touches the end of my nose.

'Hey!' I protest. 'What was that for?'

'Just because,' Eden teases. 'The world needs more yellow paint . . .'

'You could be right,' I say. 'Miss Smith is going to love this. The paint might not last forever, but it really brings the light in. Just imagine looking out at all that sunshine yellow on a grey November day!'

'As long as she doesn't think we're vandals.' Eden frowns. 'She seems a bit out of sorts today.'

Miss Smith has chosen not to come outside to sit in the sun. She's in her chair by the window, huddled in her blue shawl as if the August day is somehow chilly and forbidding. Now, as I look towards the house, I see her head has fallen against the chair; she's sleeping.

'She won't think that,' I say with confidence. 'She'll be pleased. She's got something really cool to look out on now.'

'The dead tree bugs me a bit,' Eden comments.

'Me too. We could come over tomorrow and try to do something with it.'

Eden shakes her head. 'Not tomorrow. I'm busy!'

I blink. 'OK. Right. Well, no worries.'

Eden prods me gently in the ribs with her elbow. 'Aren't you going to ask me why?' she demands. 'Why I'm busy? Go on!'

I sigh. 'Why are you busy, Eden?' I echo.

Her face lights up. 'I'm meeting Hasmita!' she exclaims. 'We're going shopping. How cool is that?'

I laugh. 'Very cool,' I admit. 'Seriously, that's brilliant news! D'you think she'll meet up with me sometime, too?'

'Of course,' Eden says. 'Maybe we really can put the Heart Club back together again! That would be amazing!'

'But Eden . . .'

'Shhh,' she laughs, putting a paint-smudged finger against my lips. 'Oh – oops!'

I retaliate, printing a fingerprint of yellow on her chin, and she laughs and streaks my cheeks with yellow, adding spots of paint above my eyebrows.

I strike back with streaks of paint across her cheek-bones, but suddenly she stops laughing and looks stricken, lost.

'What's wrong?' I ask. 'I didn't mean anything, Eden. I thought . . .'

She shakes her head. 'It's not you, Ryan,' she says. 'I was just thinking about Andie, y'know? We met at nursery, you probably remember – she painted my face with yellow paint. The two of us ended up covered in the stuff. I was just thinking . . . well, she'd have loved this.'

I bite my lip. 'She probably would have,' I say uncertainly.

'She told me I looked like sunshine,' Eden whispers.

'You do,' I say.

She leans over and kisses me, and in spite of the yellow paint she tastes like sunshine, too.

## 42

## **Eden**

If clothes shopping were a GCSE subject, Hasmita would get an A* grade. She has a knack of picking out cool, quirky items that look brilliant and don't cost the earth. Instead of being an ordeal, the shopping trip is fun. Hasmita buys fancy shades and a floppy straw hat and I get a T-shirt, a teal-blue pinafore dress with a sixties vibe and a cute little vest top that will be perfect for sunny days.

I'm on a high, buoyed up by new clothes and old friends and the memory of a kiss that turned my insides upside down. Hasmita and I chat non-stop. Any last vestiges of awkwardness have fallen away, and we're talking about anything and everything. Almost.

I tell her that I chose to ditch the whole friendship game, and Hasmita looks shocked. 'Isn't there anyone you could pal up with at Moreton Park?' she asks. I tell her I'm friends with Ryan again, then mention Chloe, Flick and Ima.

'They're lovely,' I explain. 'We had fun at Lara's party, and we've texted a few times since, but I'm scared to risk getting close to anyone again.'

'Except me,' Hasmita teases. 'And Ryan, maybe . . .'

I laugh. 'Well, OK,' I say. 'I can trust you two. We may have hurt each other in the past, let each other down, but there were reasons for that. We were just trying to cope the best way we could.'

Hasmita tells me that she found it hard to settle in at St Bernadette's but made good friends eventually.

'You have to let people in again, Eden,' she says. 'What's the alternative? Shutting down, trusting nobody, being alone? That's no way to live. Friendship is always a risk, and no, we'll probably never have anything as wonderful as the Heart Club was, but you can't make your life into some kind of shrine to the past. Give new friends a chance!'

I force a smile, even though I'm feeling wobbly.

'But, Hazz, what if I get hurt again?'

She sighs. 'You will get hurt again, Eden,' she says. 'It's normal, it's natural. It's pretty much unavoidable. Getting hurt is a side effect of being alive!'

She links my arm, rests her cheek against mine.

'I'm sorry I hurt you, Eden,' she says. 'I made a lot of mistakes, but it gets better, I promise. I will do my very best not to hurt you again, OK? I'm on your side, always.'

Hasmita drags me into the nearest cafe and orders milkshakes and chocolate brownies. 'Medicinal purposes,' she tells me. 'Chocolate brownies cure all known heartaches!'

The conversation drifts on to safer ground. She tells me how much she hates the St Bernadette's uniform, how she campaigned to get the hideous tan tights replaced by black opaques. She failed, but achieved a compromise of optional white ankle socks. She's also started a school debating group and has fallen for the brother of one of her classmates.

I tell her that I'm sort of seeing Ryan, and she whoops out loud when I tell her I kissed him.

'Wow!' she says. 'You and Ryan? Andie liked him too, didn't she?'

Guilt prickles my skin and I can't meet Hasmita's eyes, but she sees my panic and squeezes my hand.

'Look, we can't live in the past, Eden,' she says. 'That was then and this is now, and you and Ryan are perfect for each other. How about we drag him out for a milk-shake one day soon? I can't believe what you said about him turning bad boy. Ryan hasn't got a bad bone in his body.'

'He's just angry, I think,' I say. 'You know how it is; we all get by the best way we can. Hey, remember Andie's paper-crane phase? Ryan made me this . . .'

I take the crumpled paper crane from my pocket and hold it out to Hasmita, grinning.

'Oh, wow,' she says. 'So many memories! He likes you, Eden. That's cool!'

'He's still a big softy underneath,' I say. 'Remember how he always wanted a dog called Rocket? He's got one, now! So cute!'

'No way!' Hasmita laughs. 'It would be great to catch up. By the way, you got me thinking. I wrote to Tasha. I figured that shutting bits of your past away and pretending they didn't happen is not a great way to live. So hey, I'm trying. Writing to Tasha was a start – maybe she'll reply, who knows?'

'Maybe she will,' I say.

I wish I could pull Andie back into the group too, but my last few text messages have gone unanswered. Andie has vanished again. I know that hassling her with messages won't help; she'll be in touch again in her own time.

I hope.

I push away my thoughts of Andie and I'm clowning about trying on Hasmita's sunglasses and floppy hat when someone calls my name. I peer over the shades and see Ima, Chloe and Flick making their way over, and for once I am happy to see them.

'Eden! I knew it was you!' Chloe says, swiping away the floppy hat. 'Wow. I still haven't got used to your hair like that. It's gorgeous! What's with the hat and shades, though? Are you in disguise?'

'Incognito,' Hasmita giggles. 'Hi, I'm Eden's friend, Hasmita.'

'Hi!' my classmate says. 'I'm Chloe and this is Ima and Flick.'

'We have been so worried about you,' Ima breaks in. 'You

just literally vanished from Lara's party. What happened? I was worried!'

I force a grin. 'Oh I was fine; I told you. No big deal!'

This sounds lame, I know, the kind of excuse I've used a million times to keep Chloe, Flick and Ima at arm's length. Spots of pink appear on my cheeks as if to flag up the lie. It hasn't taken long for my new, reinvented self to crumble.

I've reckoned without Hasmita, though.

'You didn't tell them?' my old friend says, hands on hips. 'Seriously? You have to, Eden! It's *so* romantic!'

'A boy?' Flick shrieks. 'Not . . . Ryan Kelly?'

'No way!' Ima says, horrified. 'He was asking about you before the party, and then he stuck to you like glue while the band were playing. Just tell me you are not dating the javelin psycho of Moreton Park Academy!'

'Unreal,' Chloe breathes.

Hasmita laughs. 'Eden,' she says. 'You can't keep this a secret! C'mon, guys, grab yourselves some drinks and come and join us; we'll tell you the whole story!'

An hour later, we're all still there, trading stories and making our milkshakes last forever. I've confessed all about

Ryan, or almost all – I keep trying to tell them he's misunderstood, and that the javelin thing was wildly exaggerated, but I'm not sure they believe a word.

'It's like a fairy tale,' Flick sighs. 'Bad boy meets shy girl and changes his ways; how cool?'

'It's not really like that,' I argue.

'It's a bit like that,' Hasmita insists. 'So, girls, what have you been up to? Shopping, like us?'

'No, we've been at drama club,' Chloe says. 'It's every Monday and Friday in the holidays, and every Friday night during term time. It's fun!'

'Ooh, we should do that!' Hasmita says to me. 'I love drama, and they don't do it at St Bernadette's! Is it too late to join?'

It turns out that the club is looking for someone to help with make-up and scenery, and that anyone can lend a hand.

'Couldn't be more perfect,' Hasmita declares. 'I'm a genius with lipstick and eyeliner, right? And you've done scenery stuff before, Eden. It's a great excuse to meet up regularly, too. I think we should go!'

I am pretty sure it's also a plot to throw me together with

Chloe, Flick and Ima, but after hanging out with them today I think that might be fun. The Heart Club is over, but maybe something else can take shape from its ashes?

Friends . . . whether I am ready for them or not, they're finding their way back into my life.

## 44

# Ryan

I'm whistling as I fix myself Weetabix and pour out ice-cool orange juice, and Dad looks up from his iPad and raises an eyebrow.

'You're in a good mood again today,' he comments, as if not quite believing it. 'One of those mornings, huh? Up and at 'em, son!'

Mum is less obvious, grinning at me as she butters toast and makes coffee. I've seen the worry lift away from her shoulders these last few days, replaced by a spark of hope, of relief. It's easier to see those things than the anxiety and fear that usually cloud her expression whenever I'm around.

I pour them both a glass of orange juice and clink glasses with Mum, and Dad joins in with the whistling. The mood in the Kelly family kitchen is lighter than it has been in a very long time.

I am in a good mood. I have been for days. Eden has ended the no-touch rule and we have moved from being platonic friends to something more. The something more involves hand-holding and hugs and occasional kisses, and whether they involve yellow paint or not, the kisses are all pure sunshine.

It was almost worth losing Eden for two years just to find her again, because being with her takes away the hurt I've struggled with for so long. I can feel the hard knot of anger inside me softening, loosening. The knot is coming undone, and though the idea of that has always terrified me before, it feels OK. Without anger, other feelings will flood in, and some of them will be hard to bear, but perhaps it's time to face them.

I can see Eden waking up too, chipping away the icy shell she has hidden behind for so long. If she can do it, I can do it.

My running is not so much an anger remedy as fun these

days; Eden has been running with me a few times and says I'm brilliant.

'Properly brilliant,' she said the last time, meaning it. 'You should train, enter races, do it seriously. There's a club at school, y'know!'

'I don't do clubs,' I told her.

'I think you should do this one,' Eden said. 'Show them there's more to you than javelins and report cards. Show them you're good at something. Show yourself that you are!'

I said I'd think about it.

I don't much care what the teachers think about me, but running; maybe that would be cool. Maybe.

Most days now I take Rocket and run up to Miss Smith's house to feed the fish and water the plants, but I haven't actually seen the old lady for a while. There's no sign of her today either. I knock on the door but there's no reply – no sound at all from inside. I press my face against the dirt-streaked window, scanning past the empty armchair to the chaotic sitting room beyond. Books and newspapers are piled up in corners, ornaments crowd the shelves and side tables, dirty plates and empty cups are perched all around and the blue knitted shawl lies abandoned on the carpet.

Unease seeps through me and I push it away, impatient. Maybe she's just sleeping in? Maybe she's gone away for a few days, to stay with family? Rocket whimpers and presses his head against my leg, and I promise myself I'll come back later, with Eden, to check that everything is OK.

In the end, though, I forget, because Eden texts and tells me to come to the coffee shop in town, that afternoon at four.

**What's going on?** I ask. **Is everything OK?**

**Everything is more than OK**, she says. **See you later!**

## 44

## Eden

On Monday, something amazing happens; Tasha rings
from France. It turns out that she got not just my letter, but
one from Hasmita too, and even a postcard from Ryan.

'It had a picture of a cheese and pineapple pizza on it,'
she tells me. 'That boy is seriously deranged.'

'Seriously,' I agree.

'I thought you'd forgotten me,' she says.

'I thought *you* had!'

There is silence, apart from a slight crackling on the
line. 'We didn't have Internet for ages,' she explains. 'We
do now, though. We got new email addresses and I sent

you a whole bunch of emails to tell you, but you never replied.'

'I didn't get any emails!' I argue. 'Oh, hang on; we changed our provider last year, when we updated our broadband. We got new email addresses too.'

'That explains it,' she says. 'I thought – well, it doesn't matter. Everything will be OK now!'

There was another silence then, because of course, some things will never be OK again.

'I'm sorry I couldn't be there for you,' Tasha says, eventually. 'I didn't know what to say. That summer. It didn't seem real . . .'

'It was real,' I say with a sigh. 'But I know what you mean.'

'How are the others?' she wants to know. 'I'm going to call them too, but I wanted to speak to you first. I couldn't believe it when I read your letter, and Hasmita's, and Ryan's postcard. I got it all so wrong. I thought that you guys would stick together, help each other through. I didn't think you'd need me.'

'We'll always need you,' I tell her. 'Always. And we didn't stick together – we fell apart. Things are changing, though. We're connecting again, all of us. We can help each other now!'

'We won't be the Heart Club any more,' Tasha points out. 'It'll be different.'

'Different is good,' I say. 'The Heart Club is over.'

It doesn't feel like the end of something, though. It feels like a beginning.

Tasha and I hatch a plan, and that afternoon Ryan, Hasmita and I meet up in town. We grab a window table in our favourite cafe and Ryan orders hot chocolates with whipped cream and marshmallows all round, even though it's August. Hot chocolate was always one of Andie's favourites.

I feel a pang of guilt as I think of Andie – she still hasn't texted, and it's days since I've texted her, or even thought of her. Shame seeps through me. I've loved hanging out with Ryan, Hasmita, Chloe, Flick and Ima, and I'm thrilled to have made contact with Tasha, but I didn't mean to forget about Andie.

Ryan has smuggled a packet of Jammie Dodgers into the cafe and shares them out under the table, and we talk about a million things. About how strict the teachers are at St Bernadette's, and how Ryan holds the school record for the most detentions in one term at Moreton Park Academy, and how we should all meet up soon for a long bike ride with a picnic at the end of it.

And then I open my laptop and click on Skype. I ring through to Tasha and a few minutes later the three of us are clustered around the computer and a big picture of Tasha comes up on the screen.

'Oh wow!' she yelps. 'Oh, wow, wow, wow! It is *so* good to see you guys!'

Tasha looks so grown-up, so cool, so French, I suppose. She doesn't act cool, though. The whole time we're talking, she squeals and laughs and bounces around, the way she used to.

Hasmita is shy to start with, ashamed at not even having tried to contact the girl who was once her very best friend, but none of us are judging here. We've all made big mistakes, acted badly, messed up. We all know why.

If we can't forgive and forget, who can?

'You will have to come out here!' Tasha exclaims. 'All of you! October half-term, maybe. Or next summer! We can plan it. You can camp in the garden . . . and help me with my summer jobs, and meet my friends, and just . . . I don't know, just have fun!'

'Sounds good,' Hasmita says.

'Sounds awesome,' I correct her.

'Sounds like a plan.' Ryan grins. 'And you can come over here too. It's time we had a proper reunion!'

I can see the pieces falling into place again, the muddles and misunderstandings cleared up, swept away. It will take time, and it won't be perfect, but it's a start.

It's not until later, walking home through the park, that Ryan tells me he hasn't seen Miss Smith for a few days. Instantly I feel guilty. I've been so wrapped up in finding Hasmita and Tasha again that I have neglected the little old lady, abandoned Fish and Chips.

'Are you worried?' I ask. 'Should we call the police? Speak to the neighbours?'

'I'm sure she's OK,' Ryan says. 'I just think we should go over tomorrow and check. It's probably just coincidence; or maybe I'm calling too early. I usually go when I'm out with Rocket for a morning run.'

'Tomorrow is good,' I reply, fingers curling round the

creased paper crane in my jacket pocket. 'Plus, I had an idea for how to make that old wreck of a tree look better. You'll like it. Paper cranes!'

His face lights up. 'We could hang them from the branches,' he says. 'I'm quite quick at making them. I could probably make twenty or thirty before tomorrow, if I really tried.'

'I can beat that,' I tell him. 'I've got almost three hundred done, made from bright origami paper. It'll look fantastic!'

'Cool,' Ryan says. 'Plus, we have a string of solar-powered fairy lights in the garage. I'll bring them too. We'll go round about half-ten, then?'

'Do you really think she's OK?' I ask.

'I hope so,' Ryan says. 'It's probably nothing, only I don't think she has any immediate family looking out for her. She's a "miss", isn't she? No children, no grandchildren.'

I bite my lip.

'She's got us,' I say, and I hope that's enough.

## 45

## **Ryan**

The next morning we knock at the side door, but nobody answers.

'It doesn't mean anything,' Eden says. 'She might be in the bedroom or the bathroom. It's still quite early. Give her time.'

I haven't seen Miss Smith for six days now, but I can't say that out loud – it sounds too scary. Instead, I peer through the window and see the same cups and plates in the same places as yesterday, the same blue shawl lying on the floor. I have a bad feeling about this.

'Let's get started on the tree,' Eden is saying. 'Just wait till she gets up and comes to the window and sees it. She'll love it!'

So we decorate the tree, because I want to believe that everything is still going to be OK, that happy endings can happen to ordinary people if you want them badly enough.

I drape the solar-powered fairy lights through the bare branches, tilt the little solar reflectors upwards to the light. Eden's paper cranes are folded from patterned paper in rainbow colours, neatly strung together in hanging garlands of ten, and I loop them over the wizened branches while Eden takes a needle and thread and starts threading my own, less colourful cranes together.

'If she doesn't appear by the time we're finished, I think we should speak to the neighbours,' I say. 'Just to be on the safe side. OK?'

'OK,' Eden agrees. 'Don't worry, though. I bet she's just late getting up. Or maybe a neighbour has taken her out to the shops.'

She's still speaking when a flash silver car pulls up at the gate. A young man in a too-tight suit gets out, carrying some kind of wooden pole with a sign attached. He marches in through the gate, pushes the pole into a corner of flower bed and begins to hammer it home.

'Hey!' I yell. 'What are you doing?'

The man just about jumps out of his skin.

'Oi!' he shouts. 'Clear off, you kids! We don't want any vandalism here – this house is for sale!'

I go cold all over.

'What d'you mean, the house is for sale?' Eden challenges. 'What about Miss Smith? Where will she go?'

The man just laughs. 'Bit late to worry about the old lady now,' he says. 'She's gone. She had a fall last week – she's in hospital, and once she's on the mend she'll be moved into a nursing home. Broken hip, I think they said. She's not fit enough to live on her own, not any more. In her nineties, she is, apparently. Her nephew has put the house on the market. They'll need to sell to pay the nursing home fees.'

'Which nursing home?' I demand.

'I'm not at liberty to say!'

'We're her friends,' Eden cuts in. 'We want to visit her!'

But the man just tells us we're trespassing on private property and if we don't push off he'll ring the police.

## 46

### Eden

We sneak back to Miss Smith's house at midnight with a bucket, a torch and a plan to rescue Fish and Chips.

'They're ours, technically,' Ryan whispers, as we turn into Bennetts Lane. 'We bought them for Miss Smith, and if she's gone then they go back to being ours. We'll just have to get a fish tank, that's all.'

'It's all my fault,' I say. 'I promised I'd come every day to see Miss Smith and I didn't. I was going to make her cakes and everything, but I got sidetracked with finding Hasmita and Tasha.'

'Not your fault,' Ryan says firmly. 'You were doing what had to be done. I was here every day to feed the fish, and

I didn't see Miss Smith in all that time, so technically it was my fault. I knew something didn't feel right, but I kept telling myself it would be OK.'

'Maybe we're both to blame.' I say.

'Maybe neither of us are,' Ryan counters. 'Not everything that happens is somebody's fault; sometimes bad things happen and there's nothing anyone can do about it.'

I blink. There's an ache of sadness in my throat that threatens to unravel me. Tears sting my eyes, but of course, I never cry; I'm glad the darkness hides my face. *Sometimes bad things happen . . .*

We open the gate and my torch beam swoops over the looming shape of a skip that has pitched up on the driveway since our visit this morning. The skip is piled high with what looks like rubbish. I imagine furniture and clothes and anything in good shape will be taken to charity shops or hauled away to be sold, but all the rest, the everyday bits and pieces of a life, have been dumped.

In the torchlight, I catch a glimpse of the old deckchair I'd set up for Miss Smith to sit in the sun, chucked out like junk, the blue knitted shawl wedged behind it. I tug at the shawl. Maybe, if we can find out where Miss Smith is, we could take it to her. I remember the way her fingers used to stroke the soft wool, hugging it round her as if to ward off the cold even on the hottest days.

As I pull the shawl free, a big brown envelope is dislodged too, and falls on to the drive. I pick it up and shine the torch beam across it. In faded ink, I see the name Peter John Smith written in one corner.

'Ryan, look,' I say. 'I wonder if this is the Peter that Miss Smith kept thinking was you?'

'What's inside?'

I slide a few papers and a handful of creased photographs out of the envelope. The pictures are a timeline of some-body's life; a baby wrapped in a knitted shawl, a toddler clutching a handmade toy rabbit, a boy in a sleeveless pull-over and short trousers with his arms around a black and white mongrel. The last picture shows a teenager with unruly dark hair and a cheeky grin, sitting beside a garden pond with the dog at his side.

'No wonder she mistook you for Peter,' I breathe. 'You look just like him – and this must be Patch! Who was Peter, d'you think? What happened to him?'

Ryan takes the papers from my hands and scans through them in the torchlight. A birth certificate, dated 1945, for Peter John Smith, mother Elsa Smith of 41 Bennetts Lane; father not named.

Miss Smith had a child out of wedlock, a war child, when she was just a teenager herself. How did she manage to keep her son in an era when unmarried mothers were often forced to give up their babies for adoption? She must have loved him very much. Did her parents stand by her, support her? Was 41 Bennetts Lane her family home? Who was Peter's father; was he married to someone else, or did he die in the last few months of the war?

They are questions we will probably never know the answers to.

Ryan sifts through school reports, a certificate awarded for excellence in running, a faded birthday card signed by Peter in the wobbly, uncertain handwriting of a small child.

'Look, Eden,' Ryan whispers. 'Look . . .'

The last of the papers is a death certificate; Peter John Smith died of TB in 1959, aged fourteen.

Something shifts inside me. Unwanted thoughts flood into my head – bad thoughts, sad thoughts. I push them away again, but my heart is racing and I feel physically sick.

'Are you OK, Eden?' Ryan asks, and I square my shoulders, come back to reality.

'They threw all this away as if it was rubbish!' I say angrily. 'Miss Smith's most precious memories, chucked out with cartons of curdled milk and packets of food long past their sell-by date! It's wrong, Ryan! Peter was her only son; he should count for more than this!'

I glance at the picture of Peter as a baby again, and suddenly I understand why Miss Smith was so attached to the pale blue shawl in my hands. It's the baby shawl in the photograph.

'Ryan,' I say. 'We have to take these things to Miss Smith, at the hospital. We have to!'

'You're right,' Ryan says. 'We do.'

We leave the empty bucket on the driveway, lift a couple of paper-crane garlands from the old tree and set off to walk to the hospital. The darkened streets are silent and it's chilly now, so I wrap the shawl round me for warmth and think about the days when it was wrapped round someone different, wrapped tightly to keep out the cold and the harsh words of the world.

'They'll never let us in,' I say. 'It's past midnight. Way past visiting time . . .'

'We'll find a way,' Ryan promises. 'Trust me.'

Somehow, I do.

## 47

# Ryan

It's not that I plan to steal a wheelchair, more that one happens to materialize right in front of me. The occupant, a man with a plaster cast on his leg, has levered himself out to sit on a bench and smoke with couple of disreputable characters from the accident and emergency waiting room.

I walk confidently up to the abandoned wheelchair and steer it towards A&E, and Eden falls into step beside me, jumping into the chair just as I march through the double doors. A&E is absolute chaos at this time of night, and that has to be to our advantage, but I can only guess at which doors are code-protected and which ones aren't. I walk confidently past the reception desk and stop to talk to a nurse who is marking things on a clipboard.

'Is it left to X-ray?' I ask.

'Through the blue door, turn right, second left,' she says without looking up. 'Have you got your form?'

'Right here,' I say brightly, waving Peter Smith's school report from 1955 in the air. 'Thank you!'

She leans across distractedly and punches in the door code, and we sail through. We turn left instead of right, find the lifts and stop to study the ward plan next to them. 'Where would she be, d'you think?' I puzzle. 'Orthopaedic, maybe, with a broken hip. Or Acute Geriatric? Both on the third floor. Here we go . . .'

The lift hauls us upwards, spills us out into a deserted, brightly lit corridor that smells of disinfectant and despair.

'Which one first?' Eden asks. 'Orthopaedic? I'm not sure I pass as geriatric, even with a shawl on.'

We try the double door to Orthopaedic but it's locked and requires a keyed-in password. We push on towards Acute Geriatric, trying to think up a plausible excuse to blag our way in, but an orderly comes out through the

273

double doors pushing a trolley as we approach, and as if by magic we slide in before the doors swing shut.

'Where now?' Eden whispers.

The ward is in partial darkness except for the nurses' station at the far end. We slink along in the shadows, checking every room. Luck is on our side because we find Miss Smith in single room half way along. She's on an IV drip, her face paper-white and strained in the dim light. Various electrodes link up to a little blue monitor screen that bleeps and purrs sporadically, and her bed has metal rails along the side to stop her falling out.

I don't know exactly what I thought someone with a broken hip might look like, but Miss Smith looks way worse. She seems weary, worn out, like she's given up the fight. I don't know what to say or what to do, but Eden is leaning over now, placing the soft blue shawl in Miss Smith's twig-like arms and tucking the brown envelope under the coverlet.

Her eyes flicker open.

'Edie,' she says, and then her eyes flicker past Eden to me. 'Peter! I've been waiting for you! I've been waiting so long!'

'Shhh, shhh. I'm here now,' I whisper. 'I'm never far away, I promise.'

'Wait for me, Peter,' the old lady says. 'Wait for me. I'll be home soon.'

Miss Smith's eyes flutter shut again and when it seems clear that she's sleeping, Eden blows a kiss into the darkness and hangs a couple of paper crane garlands along the bed's side rails. We abandon the wheelchair in a corner and slip out of the room, out of the ward and into the night.

'Will she die, do you think?' Eden asks in a small voice.

'I don't know,' I say. 'She's in her nineties. She looks so frail, but she was talking about going home.'

'That's not going to happen,' Eden says. 'Some nephew who doesn't even live here is putting her into a nursing home. She won't know anyone – she won't be able to look outside and remember things from long ago.'

'Maybe that's not what she meant about being home soon,' I say softly. 'Maybe home is where Peter is?'

'How will we know?' Eden says. 'How will we find out?'

'I'll ring. If she gets better, I'll find out where they send her. Promise. We did the right thing, Eden, tonight. We did a good thing.'

'Yeah, I think we did.'

She slips her hand into mine as we walk away.

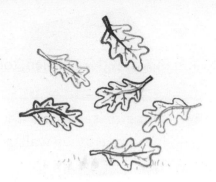

## 48

## **Eden**

All night the memories have been pushing their way into my head; flashes of things I have tried to bury for too long. The past is rearing up again, smashing through the walls I have carefully built round it, ready to break everything to bits . . . my heart, my mind, my sanity.

Ryan is rescuing the goldfish while I sit under the ancient tree in Miss Smith's garden, fairy lights glittering above me, garlands of paper cranes rustling softly in the breeze.

When somebody old is sick or hurt and their body is worn out, there's a sense that their time is coming to an end, that death might even be a blessing. Maybe, if this is the end for Miss Smith, she will be with her son again; she'll finally be 'home'.

When somebody young dies, though, there is no sense in it at all.

'Ryan?' I say. 'We can talk about anything, can't we? Trust each other totally?'

His pale face turns towards me in the shadows.

'Sure,' he says, and there's a soft splash as he scoops the second goldfish into the bucket.

'So how come we never talk about Andie?'

There must be an edge to my voice, because Ryan puts the bucket down and runs across the grass towards me, but he is too slow, too late to stop the tide of memories.

I am falling to pieces, breaking apart. The past is rising up inside me like the monsoon after a long drought; violent, unstoppable, washing away everything in its path. Ryan's arms fold round me, holding me close, and I let myself fall against him.

I haven't cried in two years, but now I cannot stop. Fat tears run down my cheeks and my breath comes in ugly, gasping sobs. I wipe away salt tears and snot with an angry fist, but they keep coming. A kind of animal pain rises up inside me and comes pouring out; a howling, wheezing, keening sound. I cannot stop it.

I don't know how long it goes on for. It feels like forever, but it could be half an hour; it could just be minutes. All I know is that I'm exhausted, shaking, spent. I know my eyes will be red and swollen and ugly, my skin blotchy, streaked with rivulets of eyeliner, and I don't care.

I've been ignoring the truth for so long, too long. I can't fight it any more.

'Why did she have to die, Ryan?' I whisper. 'Why did Andie have to die?'

I quarrelled with Andie because of Ryan, and it was different from any other row we'd had – not that there had been many. Maybe this one would have blown over too, but we didn't get the chance to see if that would happen. Andie went on holiday to Scotland the day after the camp-out sleepover, and the angry silence deepened into something sad and sour.

I texted her non-stop for three days; grovelling apologies, promises of loyalty, bitter regrets. Silence. On the fourth day, my anger boiled over.

**Is this the kind of friendship we have?** I challenged

her. **The kind that only works when you're getting your own way? The kind that puts your feelings above mine, above everybody else's? That's not a friendship, Andie. I thought we were better than this, but I can see now that it was all one way and I don't need that in my life. I don't need you. You've smashed our friendship to pieces. I hope you're proud.**

The text made me feel better for about five minutes, and then the regrets began, but this time I was too proud to grovel. Andie had made a choice; she didn't want me in her life any more, and I pretended I didn't want her.

Ryan kept his head down through it all, but Hasmita and Tasha were distraught.

'She'll calm down,' Hasmita insisted. 'Give her time. Her pride's hurt, that's all.'

Andie had texted Tasha and Hasmita to say the Scottish beaches were beautiful and deserted, that the sun was shining. Andie was in the one place in the whole of the British Isles that was actually sunny; she was having fun while I was stuck here in the endless rain, eaten up with anger and regret. The family planned to travel home on Saturday, stopping off a few times on the way, Tasha told me. They'd be home by midnight.

'Go and see her first thing on Monday,' Tasha advised. 'You need to talk it through, clear the air. Everything will be OK, you'll see!'

But things were never OK again.

At ten that evening, just as Andie's family were driving off the M1 in torrential rain, a lorry jackknifed and skidded into them.

Andie's mum and little brothers got off with minor cuts and bruises, and her dad had a broken arm and minor head injuries. Andie, though, had been sitting on the right-hand side of the car, behind her dad. She'd taken the full force of the crash.

She was eleven years old, full of life, brimming with ideas, brave and beautiful and clever and kind. She could do a cartwheel, get ten out ten in any maths test, tell the best ghost stories, run faster than any boy I knew. She never got colds, she never got nits, she never said a mean thing in her life until the day we fell out over Ryan.

Bad things were not supposed to happen to people like Andie.

She died that night.

## 49

## Ryan

Some things you just don't see coming, and then it's too late and all you can do is try to pick up the pieces, even though you know that nothing will ever be the same again. That was how it was when Andie died. We were in shock, all of us, and instead of sticking together we fell apart. I tried to talk to Eden, but I could see she was numb, her feelings buried deep beneath a thick layer of permafrost. Her eyes had been blank, as if she didn't even know who I was.

I wondered if she blamed me; I thought she probably did.

The rain lashed down all through the funeral, as if the

heavens were crying. The coffin was small and made of golden-coloured wood, heaped high with white wreaths. The smell of flowers was so heady, so strong, that even now I can't stand that smell. It brings back the pain.

So many bad things.

Andie's dad, with his head bandaged, his arm in plaster, was sobbing. Andie's mum broke down and had to be taken out of the church. So many people, cramming the pews, the aisles, crowding outside the church under black umbrellas. Did they all feel as broken inside as I did?

So much black, too. Black suits, black ties, black dresses, black hats. Andie would have hated that; she was all about colour and sunshine, after all. The girls wore the brightest clothes they could find, pink and purple and emerald green, and I wore bright blue jeans and a red sweatshirt.

I think that would have made Andie smile.

After the funeral was over, the clouds rolled away and the sun finally came out for the first time in weeks and weeks, but it was a thin, watery kind of sunshine.

Well, it was a thin, watery kind of world, without Andie.

Andie's dad came up to me after the funeral and handed me the Harry Potter book I'd lent her to read on holiday;

I'd never know now if she'd liked it or not. I put it back on the shelf, but I knew I'd never look at those books again. It was like they belonged to someone else, a kid who had had the world at his feet, a kid with high hopes and big dreams of a world where anything was possible.

I wasn't that kid any more.

It's crazy, I know, but after the first shock wore off, after the tears and the nightmares and the funeral, I got angry. Why Andie? It made no sense at all.

Andie was the first friend I ever had, my best friend, and now she was gone. After a couple of months, her family put their house on the market and moved north to Scotland. They said there were too many memories here, that they needed a fresh start. They went back to the town they'd holidayed in; they said it was the last place Andie had been really happy. A new family moved in next door; a family with two little girls who rampaged around the garden whooping, shrieking and laughing. It was a strange kind of torture to listen to that.

The rest of the Heart Club melted away as if it had never existed at all. Tasha and her parents packed up and drove to France, shell-shocked, the day after the funeral.

I emailed her a couple of times, but I didn't hear back. Nothing.

Hasmita put on that bottle-green blazer and tartan skirt, drew a line under her childhood and refused to cross it. I'd see her sometimes, in town with her new friends, arms full of books. Mostly, she didn't even notice me, but once our eyes met and she waved awkwardly and hurried on to catch up with her friends.

Eden turned herself into someone I barely recognized, a grey, silent shadow of the girl she used to be. I saw her that first day, her golden-brown hair dyed black, her uniform several sizes too big, looking like she wanted to hide inside its folds, and I didn't even know it was her. If she wanted to be invisible, well, it was working.

Me? I had no strategy at all for handling the hurt, and slowly my grief hardened into anger.

My parents took me to the RSPCA kennels and we picked out a black and white mongrel puppy that looked exactly like the dog I'd been doodling and drawing all those years; the dog I'd campaigned so hard to have. I called him Rocket and sometimes, late at night, I held him close and cried into his fur, but still the anger remained.

Some days I woke up filled with it; some days it spilled out of me at school and I found myself yelling at teachers, scrapping with classmates, kicking walls, committing small acts of insolence and defiance. Nobody understood; I didn't think anyone ever could, but it turned out I was wrong about that.

Eden sits beside me in the quiet darkness, her face tilted up to the black velvet sky as if watching the stars. In the silvery glow from the fairy lights I can see the scatter of freckles on her upturned nose, the glint of tears on her pale cheeks.

'How long does it take for this to stop hurting?' she asks, her voice soft.

I tell her I don't know.

## 50

## Eden

Ryan walks me home through the pink and gold daybreak, and we talk about Andie; about how wonderful it was to know her, how devastating it was to lose her, how messed up we've been ever since. It turns out it wasn't just tears I'd been bottling up for so long; it was memories too – happy ones, sad ones, silly ones. They all come tumbling out, a tangle of life and love and sadness, and I wonder how I have survived for two years without talking about Andie, without having Ryan by my side.

'Do you remember when we used to tell ghost stories at Halloween?' I ask him now. 'How Andie used to say that if she ever died young, she'd come back and haunt us? I've thought of that over and over, these last two years.'

'Me too,' Ryan says. 'I'd have given anything to see her – just once, to say goodbye. We didn't get the chance, did we?'

I shake my head, tears starring my lashes.

We didn't get the chance to say goodbye, and we didn't get the chance to patch up the first serious bump in the road our friendship ever hit. We didn't get the chance to part as friends.

'Do you believe in ghosts?' I ask now.

'No,' Ryan says. 'I wish I did.'

I take a deep breath and try to find the words to tell him about Andie; about how she'd vanished in the park when Ryan came along, how she'd slipped away from the party before I could say goodbye. I can't work out how to say it, where to start.

Would he even believe me? Would he be hurt that Andie had come back to see me, but not him?

Andie breezed back into my life and turned it upside down. In typical Andie style, she sorted out my wardrobe, nudged me out of my solitude, helped me find the courage to reach out to Ryan and Hasmita and Tasha. Didn't she?

Doubt floods through me suddenly. Was any of it real?

The mind plays tricks on us, tells us what we want to hear, shows us what we want to see. Would it be such a big leap for me to dream up a scenario where Andie came back, told me she was sorry, told me to get a grip?

I hug Ryan goodnight at the gate and let myself into the flat, creep up the stairs and into my room. In the shadows the room looks peaceful, calm; two pillows beneath the duvet mimicking a sleeping body. Well . . . enough to fool my mum, anyway.

Did I imagine it all? I don't know what to think any more.

I crawl under the covers, pull the duvet over my head and fall into sleep.


A hail of gravel clatters against my window, waking me just after two in the afternoon, and I go to the window, bleary eyed. Ryan waves at me from the path, Rocket at his side. The goldfish bucket is on the path beside him, and his face is lit up with the biggest grin I've ever seen.

'Come down!' he yells. 'Wait till you see!'

I clatter down the stairs and open the door, and Ryan is on the doorstep grinning.

'You brought the goldfish to see me?' I ask, baffled.

'Only briefly,' he says. 'Listen, this morning, when I woke up, I was thinking about Andie. I couldn't get her out of my head, and something made me take down that Harry Potter book I lent to her to take to Scotland. Do you remember? Her dad gave it back to me at the funeral, but I've never been able to look at it until now.'

'So?'

'Just look,' Ryan says. 'Look inside!'

He opens the book and inside the front cover there is Andie's handwriting, as lively and vivid as she once was. *Loved the book, Ryan. Bad news; now you'll have to lend me the others! Sorry I was such a drama queen at the camp-out – what can I say? I'm an idiot! Forgive me?*

'No way,' I breathe. 'That's amazing, Ryan! So weird!'

'That's not all,' he says. 'Look what else there was.'

He hands me a letter. My name is written on the envelope in silver gel pen in a strong, looping handwriting I know better than my own.

'I'm going to go,' Ryan says. 'Give you some space, OK? Because this is kind of a big deal, right? But whatever the letter says . . . Well, I'm here for you, Eden.

I promise. I'll text you – or you text me, if you need me. See you later!'

He picks up the bucket, heads along the path and walks briskly along the road, Rocket at his heels.

My fingers shake as I open the envelope, draw out the pages, I sit down on the doorstep in the afternoon sun and begin to read.

## 52

## **Andie**

*Dear Eden,*

*Oh, it sounds so stupid being all formal and serious. We don't really do serious, and we definitely don't do fights and fall-outs and long, long silences. What can I say? I was really out of order at the sleepover. Over-the-top. Mean, spiteful, grade-A bitch. I don't know why I said those things really. I was just so hurt.*

*I was so sure that would be the night me and Ryan got together, and . . . well, it wasn't. I saw you slip and hurt your ankle, but I didn't care because I wanted to keep on dancing with Ryan. I pretended not to see. And of course Ryan stopped dancing and went* to help you and I was so, so angry. I tried not to care, I really did, but I was jealous. I think I knew all along that Ryan had a crush on you. I'd just pushed it to the back of my mind, blocked it out.

I knew you wouldn't flirt with Ryan, anyway, because we'd talked so much about how much I liked him. I'd be lying if I said I hadn't seen the sadness in your eyes when we did that, but that was another thing I chose to push away. But yeah, I knew you liked him too.

And then I saw him try to kiss you, and I went a little bit crazy. Ryan liked you best, and deep down I knew he always had. Anger flooded through me like poison - anger and hurt. You were supposed to put me first, Eden. That's the way it's always been. I felt betrayed, and I didn't care how upset you were, that you were saying sorry, crying. It didn't matter what Hasmita, Tash or Ryan said, I couldn't back down. I watched you go home that night with a sad, sick anger. I never wanted to see you again. I pressed delete on every text you sent, told my parents I wouldn't speak to you if you rang. I was glad to be going to Scotland, because it meant I didn't have to see you, didn't have to listen to Ryan bleating about how nothing actually happened, how cruel I was being.

I won't lie, Eden. I was so, so hurt.

Scotland is awesome, by the way. The sun has shone all week and we've practically lived on the beach. I was glad at first that it's been raining back home. Serves you right, I thought. But I guess the sun has warmed me up, calmed me down. The anger isn't directed at you any more, Eden, it's directed at me. I knew you liked Ryan, knew he liked you, but I tried to control you by telling you how much I loved him, getting you to help set us up. I was relying on your loyalty to get what I wanted, and that wasn't fair. I can see that now.

Well, the whole thing backfired big time, right?

I lost you and I lost Ryan, and Hasmita and Tash aren't exactly impressed with me either right now. Mum and Dad know something's wrong because I've been so miserable all week, but I can't talk to them about it; some holiday, huh? I haven't been joining in much, just lying on the beach with Ryan's Harry Potter book, and it's brilliant, sure, but I can't even concentrate on that because I'm all mixed up, all upset.

I got your last text and I know how angry you are with me, and all I can say is that I deserve that anger. I deserve to lose you, but I really, really hope I haven't.

I feel like such an idiot, Eden.

The only person I want to talk to is you. I miss you and I know I won't have the guts to say all this on the phone, and besides, you'd have every right to cut the call or block me or whatever after all that has happened. So I'm writing it down, and if I can just get hold of a stamp and an envelope I will post it, and if not I will turn up on your doorstep the first day we're back from Scotland and deliver it in person. Even if you're mad, even if you slam the door on me, I'll make sure you get this letter.

I have been a rubbish friend, Eden, and I'm sorry. I was hurt and angry and selfish, and I didn't stop to think about you or Ryan. OK, I will find it hard if you and he start seeing each other, but you know what? I'll get over it. I will. I am not going to let this come between me and my best friends in the whole, entire world.

All I know is that I'm miserable without you, Eden.

Please say that you'll forgive me. I have been so, so stupid and I'm scared I've lost you. That can't happen, Eden, because I care about you way too much.

I'll make it right, I promise.

I'm sorry, I'm sorry, I'm sorry. Please say you'll forgive me.

Love you loads, forever and always,

Andie oxox

52

## Ryan

I rang the hospital and told them I was Miss Smith's
nephew, and they told me she'd been discharged to the
nursing home. 'Which nursing home?' I asked, and the
receptionist told me she wasn't at liberty to disclose that,
and besides, I ought to know because I'd arranged it.

I hung up and went through the Yellow Pages; I pretended
to be her great-nephew this time, and the sixth nursing
home I called told me she was just settling in but I could
visit if I liked.

I said I'd be there within the hour. I drop the letter off
with Eden, then walk across town to the Silver Bay Nursing
Home. They try to stop me bringing Rocket in, even though

I pretend he's a therapy dog, and when they spot the fish in the bucket I think they will actually throw me out. In the end one of the carers shakes her head and takes me through to see Miss Smith.

She's sitting up in bed, the blue shawl tucked round her shoulders, and she looks a lot better than she did last night. Her room is small and impersonal, but at least it's not part of a hospital ward.

'Peter!' she exclaims, her face lighting up. 'I thought I'd dreamed you! And Patch!'

'I've brought you Fish and Chips,' I say, holding out the bucket. 'From the pond? I thought you could have them in a tank. I'd get you one, only I'm all out of cash and they were much easier to carry in a bucket.'

'We can get a tank for them,' the carer offers. 'Put them in the lounge. The clients will love it!'

'Am I going home soon?' Miss Smith asks, and I tell her she is, even though it's not true.

'I'm sorry about the javelin,' I tell her. 'I didn't mean it, and I've learned my lesson. I'm going to change. I'm not hanging round with Buzz and Chris any more, and I'm going to join the running team at school.'

'Oh, you were always good at running,' Miss Smith says. 'You got a certificate!'

'Maybe I will again,' I say. 'I'll make you proud, Miss Smith – and Mum and Dad, too. I'm going to ask Mr Khan to find me a counsellor, somewhere outside school, and I'll see if I can dig the anger out and let go of it for good. Maybe Eden will do that, too. And I'm going to come to see you every week, Miss Smith, I promise you. Every week until you go home.'

'You're a good boy, Peter,' she says, and I grin, because I want to be that again, I really do.

I leave the nursing home and set off at a sprint, trying to outrun the events of last night. Paper cranes, an old lady who thinks I am her long-dead son, a goldfish kidnap, the past coming finally to the surface like the wreck of a once-great galleon, broken and terrible in its beauty.

I run and Rocket runs and we go on running until we are exhausted, until the breath burns in my chest and the muscles ache in my legs, because that way I know I'm alive, alive, alive. My feet slow to a standstill and I look up at the clear blue sky and gulp in fresh air. I'm out on the edge of town, an area I never come to. There's a big green space to one side of me, rolling grass and ancient willow trees, and across the way there's a street of shops, small and local and well looked after, including a pizzeria that says it opens at seven.

I slip through the wrought-iron gates and into the quiet, tree-lined green space, and find a place to curl up and sleep beneath the willow trees.

## 53

# Eden

A million thoughts swirl around my head, too fleeting to pin down; sadness, regret, grief, loss – and relief, too. Acceptance. It has been a long time coming. Andie didn't hate me after all; she was angry, she was jealous, she lashed out – but she was sorry. She just never got the chance to tell me that.

Two years is a long time to believe your best friend hated you, and it's a very long time to hate yourself. Something twists free inside me, sad and sharp and painful. It lifts away from my shoulders like a burden I no longer have to carry, dissolves into nothing on the late afternoon air. There is still a hole in my heart, a place that hurts, but the poison has gone and I feel brighter, braver, stronger.

Can someone reach out from beyond the grave, walk back into your life and fix things for you? Maybe, if you've been making as much of a mess of it as I was. A dead girl's fashion and friendship advice changed my life, helped put the Heart Club back together. Tasha's coming over in the October break; her parents have booked the flight, and Ryan, Hasmita and I are going to go to France next summer. Andie believed in magic, in stardust and miracles and paper cranes, but for the last two years I haven't believed in anything, not even myself. Maybe it's time to change that?

I click on my mobile, search for Andie's messages, but my inbox has no trace of any of them. Did I imagine them? Were they ever there at all? I smile, grab my jacket and head outside.

There are so many ways to say goodbye.

I take a walk through the park and watch the little kids running across the grass, playing on the swings, laughing, singing, living. I used to be like that once; maybe, just maybe, I could be again.

I pass a flower bed where someone has knocked against

some of the tall, white blooms. One lies snapped and broken on the path in front of me, petals unfurling, perfect, beautiful. It makes me think of Andie.

I pick it up and keep on walking, through the park and away from town, down less familiar streets.

I am not the kind of person who usually visits graveyards, trust me. I do not buy cheap flowers and kneel on the grass and cry. I just like to walk through sometimes, under the willow trees, where everything is green and calm and peaceful. I do not stop, I do not pray, I do not kid myself it'll make me feel any better.

It's just that sometimes it helps me to feel close to Andie.

The place is quiet, except for a few old ladies arranging flowers and fetching water from the taps. I try not to look across towards where Andie is buried, but as always, I just can't help it. So I look, and my eyes open wide.

A boy and a dog are sitting on the velvety grass beside the gravestone. The boy has unkempt wavy hair and grey eyes, and he is eating takeaway pizza straight from the box. He sees me and his cheeks flare pink, as though he has been caught smoking behind the school gym. His arm jerks upwards into a wave. 'Hey,' he says. 'Eden!'

'Ryan,' I say. 'Great minds think alike, huh?'

Rocket bounds towards me, tail waving, and I duck down to stroke his fur, hold him close, then step off the path and walk over to Ryan. He pats the ground beside him and I sink down on the daisy-scattered grass.

Without thinking, I start picking daisies, weaving them into a tiny, bracelet-sized chain, the way I used to do for Andie long ago.

'I've never visited her grave before,' he tells me. 'Stupid, right?'

'Not so stupid.' I shrug. 'I come sometimes, just to be near, but she's not here, not really, is she?'

'I don't think so, no.'

Ryan offers me a slice of pizza. It's cheese and pineapple, the kind he always ordered for Andie.

'Your favourite,' I say, knowing it really isn't. Typical Ryan, still thinking of what Andie liked, two years on.

'I could get to like it, eventually.' He frowns. 'It's just the pineapple that I'm not sure about.'

'So why not order cheese and tomato, or pepperoni, or something you do like?' I suggest.

'No, I'll stick with cheese and pineapple,' he says. 'I

expect it's an acquired taste. You can't rush these things.'

He picks the pineapple pieces off, sets them neatly along the granite plinth beneath the gravestone. I imagine the birds and squirrels coming after we've gone and eating the pineapple, leaving everything neat and tidy again.

I put the daisy-chain bracelet on the gravestone too, beside the bits of pineapple, and the broken white flower from the park. I fish the crumpled paper crane Ryan gave me weeks ago in the school library out of my pocket and sit it on the marble ledge, tweaking its wings until it looks like it could fly.

I remember Andie's paper-crane craze, remember the story of Sadako who thought that if she could just make one thousand paper cranes she would get any wish she wanted. I only made three hundred, but perhaps I got my wish after all. I got to see Andie again, make things right, make a fresh start.

'My mum comes and puts flowers here, sometimes,' Ryan tells me. 'She comes in case nobody else does, now that the family have moved away. She says that sometimes there are flowers there already. Was that you?'

'I left flowers on her birthday, once,' I say. 'And holly and mistletoe at Christmas. Once, I left Jammie Dodgers because they were her favourite.'

'Two years of trying to cope alone,' Ryan says. 'How come it took us so long to work out that it couldn't be done; that we needed each other?'

'You tell me,' I sigh.

I stretch out my fingers and touch the gravestone, trace the letters engraved on its surface. Andie isn't here, but still, I'm lucky. I had the chance to say goodbye after all, to say how much she meant to me. I had the chance to put my arms round my best friend and breathe in that sweet vanilla scent, hold her one last time.

It wasn't enough; how could it be? But still it was something.

I'd give anything to see her again, even now.

We stand up to go, and Ryan puts his hand in mine. It feels easy and natural, like we're meant to walk that way, fingers tightly entwined. The light is fading as we walk away, and the sun is setting.

I look back as we walk out through the gate, and that's when I see her, running along the grass among the gravestones, trailing a skipping rope. She is no more than four or five, a little girl in a red plastic apron, with blonde pigtails streaked with purple, pink and green. She waves, and I see the daisy-chain bracelet on her wrist, and then she turns away and is gone, lost in the lengthening shadows.

# Cathy Cassidy's
## Paper Crane Project

Japanese legend says that anyone who folds 1,000 paper cranes so pleases the gods that they are granted a wish . . .

### Sadako and the 1,000 Paper Cranes

Sadako Sasaki was a Japanese girl who lived near Hiroshima, Japan. She was just two when the atom bomb was dropped on 6 August, 1945. At the age of 11, she was diagnosed with leukaemia as a result of radiation from the bomb. Sadako's best friend told her the legend of the paper cranes and Sadako decided to fold 1,000 paper cranes to make her wish to get well come true. Sadly, she had folded a total of just 644 cranes when she died aged 12 in 1955. Sadako's friends and classmates completed the 1,000 paper cranes and these were buried with her. A statue of Sadako now stands at Hiroshima, and at its foot is a plaque which reads: *'This is our cry. This is our prayer. Peace on Earth.'*

## Make a Paper Crane:

- The paper crane is Japan's most powerful symbol of peace and hope.

- On the next page you will find a step-by-step guide to making your paper crane. **You can also Google 'make a paper crane' to find helpful videos to take you through the process.**

- It's tricky at first, but with just a little practice you'll be an expert, and ready to spread the word!

## More Ideas:

- String cranes together and make a paper crane hanging, curtain or wall
- Make cranes in rainbow colours, or with patterned paper
- What is the biggest/smallest crane you can make?
- Find out more about the story of Sadako
- Write poems/haikus inspired by the cranes

Don't forget to send in your photos at
### www.cathycassidy.com

# How to Make a Paper Crane

Begin with a large square piece of paper - one side coloured and the other plain.
In the diagrams, the shaded part represents the coloured side and the dotted lines the creases.
Remember, Google 'make a paper crane' to see a step-by-step video.

**1.**

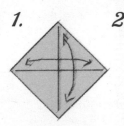

Start with a square piece of paper, coloured side up. Fold diagonally in half and open. Then fold in half the other way.

**2.**

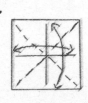

Turn the paper over to the white side. Fold in half, crease well and open. Fold again in the other direction.

**3.**

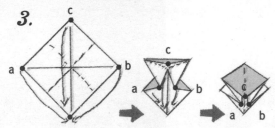

Using the creases you have made, bring corners **a** and **b** together and corner **c** down to the bottom corner. Then flatten

**4.**

Fold the top triangular flaps into the centre to make a kite shape and unfold.

**5.**

Fold the top downwards, crease well and unfold.

**6.**

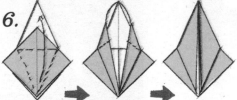

Take the bottom corner of the upper layer and pull it up, so that it forms a canoe shape. Press down firmly so that the sides of this canoe shape flatten to make a diamond shape.

**7.**

Turn the crane over and repeat **Steps 4-6** on the other side.

**8.**

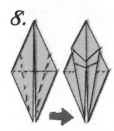

Fold the top flaps into the centre.

**9.**

Repeat on the other side.

**10.**

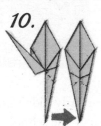

Fold both 'legs' up, crease very well and unfold.

**11.**

Fold the 'legs' inside out along the crease you just made.

**12.**

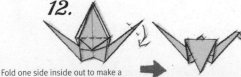

Fold one side inside out to make a head, then fold down the wings.

## Congratulations!

**Your finished paper crane!**

*Look out for another special treat from Cathy . . .*

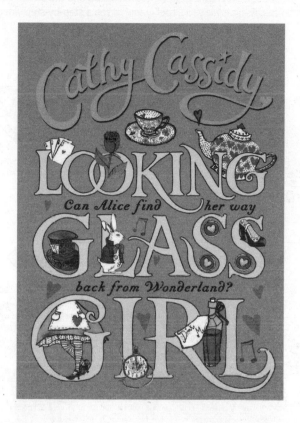

Alice nearly didn't go to the sleepover. Why would Savvy, queen of the school, invite someone like *her*?

Now Alice is lying unconcious in a hospital bed.

Lost in a world of dreams and half-formed memories, she is surrounded by voices – the doctor, her worried friends and Luke, whose kisses the night of the fall took her by surprise . . .

When the accident happened, her world vanished – can Alice ever find her way back from wonderland?

**Read the first book in Cathy Cassidy's
irresistible Chocolate Box Girls series!**

Cherry Costello's life is about to change forever. She and
Dad are moving to Somerset where a new mum and a
bunch of brand-new sisters await. And on Cherry's first
day there she meets Shay Fletcher – the kind of boy who
should carry a government health warning. But Shay
already has a girlfriend, Cherry's new stepsister, Honey.
Cherry knows her friendship with Shay is dangerous – it
could destroy everything. But that doesn't mean she's going
to stay away from him . . .

Catch all the latest
news and gossip from

Cathy Cassidy

at

**www.cathycassidy.com**

★ Sneaky peeks at new titles

★ Details of signings and events near you

★ Audio extracts and interviews with Cathy

★ Post your messages and pictures

**Don't Miss a Word!**

Sign up to receive a **FREE** email newsletter
from Cathy in your inbox!

Go to *www.cathycassidy.com*